You Again

JoAnn Ross

A book nerd, a brainiac science guy, and a misplaced killer whale...

Meghann Quinn wasn't always a hugely successful author. Adam Wayne wasn't always a marine biologist studying whales. Back in high school in Shelter Bay, Oregon, she was the shy book nerd helping the brainiac science guy pass English. Meghann had no idea Adam would turn into such a hottie. Adam has no idea their once-upon-a-time sweet summer romance inspired Meghann's popular teen novels.

Two shy geeks didn't have the courage to share their true feelings back then. But now that Meghann's back in town, they're pondering life's important questions. Such as, will Adam ask her to the Snow Ball? And what are they going to do about the lost Orca who shows up on Christmas Eve? And can two nerds get past their initial insecurity to take a second chance on a once-in-a-lifetime love?

"Destiny! Destiny! No escaping that for me!"

Young Frankenstein

1

AFTER YEARS OF waiting tables and bartending all over New York City, struggling not to dump Stoli martinis over the heads of guys who'd pat her butt, and doing temp work where she'd often be expected to appear in a business suit and heels at a moment's notice and put up with similar Neanderthal behavior, Meghann Quinn considered the ability to work at home in her pajamas one of the best perks of her job.

Today she'd changed out of her usual writing uniform of yoga pants and oversized Doctors Without Borders T-shirt to meet her editor, who also happened to be her best friend, for lunch. Having arrived early at the restaurant located in the beautiful old Metropolitan Bank building, and after being seated in the upstairs mezzanine she began browsing the web on her phone, catching up with the outside world that she'd lost track of while deep in book-deadline hell.

Five minutes later, she decided that the young adult romances she wrote—which the *New York Times Book Review* had said captured the thrills and despair of high school in all its roller coaster glory—seemed rainbow and unicorn cheery compared to world reality these days.

"Hey." A familiar voice pulled her out of a depressing op-ed piece about the number of children who were food insecure. "I'm sorry I'm late. In case you haven't noticed, everyone on the planet has come here to celebrate an iconic New York City Christmas."

Meghann put down her phone. "I thought Dickens made London the symbol of Christmas iconicity."

"*A Christmas Carol* is, indeed, iconic," Caroline Winters agreed as she sat down at the table. "And, as a publishing professional, I sincerely wish it continued to stand at the pinnacle of holiday symbolism. But if a poll were to be taken, at least in this country, I'll bet the top two winners would be *It's a Wonderful Life* and *Miracle on 34th Street*. Which, by the way, is in total gridlock. You'd think the president was in town or something."

She blew out a breath as she pulled off a pair of crimson gloves. "I finally decided I'd make better time walking."

"Through the snow? In those heels?" Although she hadn't witnessed Caro's grand entrance, Meghann figured few men in the Blue Water Grill had missed those legs, clad in black tights displayed to advantage by a thigh-length red sweater dress and over-the-knee stiletto boots. "It's amazing you even managed to make it up the stairs."

"What doesn't kill you makes you stronger," Caro said. "Though I'll admit to having a bit of trouble at Herald Square because of all the piles of frozen white stuff on the sidewalk. But proving the holiday spirit is alive in Gotham, a guy who was on his way downtown from the New York Yacht Club had his driver pull over and offered me a ride."

"Yay for chivalry."

"I know." Ignoring Meghann's dry tone, Caro dimpled prettily as she looked through the railing to the bar down below just in time to have a man who could have stepped out of a Ralph Lauren commercial lift a coffee cup in salute to her. "It doesn't hurt that he's not only sweet as pie, he's also hot."

Caro had graduated from Ole Miss, home to such disparate authors as Faulkner and Grisham. After deciding that writing involved spending too much time in your own head, she'd moved to New York and worked her way up through the publishing ranks to senior editor. Although she'd lost most of her accent, from time to time a bit of moonlight and magnolias slid into her speech.

"He'd already had lunch at the club but insisted on waiting downstairs at the bar to take me back to the office. Isn't that sweet?"

"As pie," Meghann agreed.

"He also volunteered to give you a ride."

"That's not necessary."

"I know. You're Ms. Independent."

The waiter chose that moment to arrive to take their orders. "Since nothing gets done the week before Christmas and we're having the office party this afternoon, I think I'll start celebrating early with a cranberry pomegranate martini," Caro decided.

Having finished her book, Meghann decided she'd earned a celebratory martini. "Make that two."

Although the second-floor tables afforded more privacy than downstairs, Caro leaned across the table, clearly not wanting any possible eavesdroppers to hear her. "You have to accept the ride, Meghann, because I want you to meet him. I think he may be The One. And besides, there's plenty of room. I swear, my entire apartment could fit into the back of his car."

"I'm not going to point out that as an editor, you should probably steer clear of hyperbole, but since it's started snowing again and just in case he is The One"—she put in air quotes with her fingers—"I want to check him out."

"Please tell me that you're not going to grill him the way you did Barry."

"Oh, would you be referring to the same Barry who was The One until he texted that he was breaking up with you just in case you'd failed to notice that he'd changed his status to single on Facebook? On, need I remind you Valentine's Day? Thus suggesting he probably wouldn't be showing up with roses and chocolate."

"Well, there is that."

"You're lucky to be rid of him," Meghann said. That was absolutely true. She'd never trusted the fast-talking, Armani-suited bond trader.

"I know. But Shep is nothing like that. We're going out tonight after I get off work and he even invited me to his parents' home in Greenwich for Christmas dinner."

"Shep?"

"It's short for Shepherd. He's named after his father, who was named after his grandfather, who was named after his great-grandfather. He's technically a fourth."

Which showed a decided lack of originality in the guy's family, but was still an improvement over being named for a dog breed, Meghann thought as the waiter appeared with their drinks and took their orders.

After a bit of discussion over menu items, they settled on sharing the pumpkin ravioli with side orders of orange and pomegranate salad.

"I promise I won't grill him," Meghann said once the waiter had left. *Unless absolutely necessary.*

"Thank you. And to be honest, I left the office late because although I read all night, I still had to finish reading *Leaving Lonely Town.*"

Having been about to take a drink, Meghann lowered her glass to the table. Caro might be her closest friend, but she was also a diligent editor who was excellent at looking at the entire forest on those occasions Meghann had gotten lost in the trees.

"I love it."

Meghann let out a long, relieved breath. After months of living with her fictional characters, she often grew so close to them she tended to lose perspective. "I'm glad. I know you weren't wild about the proposal."

"I liked the proposal. A lot, or I wouldn't have bought it. But I will admit to having a few qualms about Jason. I worried he could end up a stereotypical high school bad boy tempting wallflower valedictorian Heather away from the seemingly nice guy.

"But the way you flipped them, by giving wounded Jason so many more sensitivity layers than he showed to the world, and revealing outwardly nice guy Will's narcissism, (which he'd initially covered so well), worked. I actually got a little teary when, on that last page, Jason finally has his douchenosity, which, of course, he's only taken on as a defense measure, eroded by the pure power of true teenage love."

"I cried when I wrote that," Meghann admitted.

"I could tell…I do have one suggestion though."

"Oh?" Meghann took a drink of the holiday-bright martini, hoping the change wouldn't require a complete rethinking of the story she'd spent the past six months living.

"How wedded are you to the grandfather getting that transplant?"

"Well, since the notification call that a heart had become available was the only scene I knew when I started the book, I was pretty much writing toward it," Meghann admitted.

She knew many writers who plotted out their books with charts, arrows, and collages of their planned storyline. She'd tried that early on in her career and found it had only caused a huge wall between herself and her characters. Because she wrote to find out what happened, she'd learned to trust those characters to lead her through the often foggy woods and the storms that came with teenage life.

"I think letting him die would work in many ways. It would give Heather a reason to break the rest of the way out of her shy shell so she could provide support for Jason. It could also show how much more secure loving her has made him. That he can lose his grandfather, who was the only person who'd ever truly loved him…"

"Before Heather," Meghann pointed out.

"Before Heather," Caro agreed. "But in the past, when emotions threatened to penetrate that defensive shell he'd developed, he'd become outwardly even more of a bad boy. Now, while the rest of his family—who've always held themselves up as models of perfection—are greedily battling over the inheritance, it's obvious that he's the only one who truly cares that the old man has died.

"But he's also resigned to the knowledge that his grandfather lived a long and fruitful life and can now be reunited with the wife he never stopped loving. Even during all these years since her tragic passing in that plane crash."

"Because he understands that kind of forever-after love for the first time in his life." Meghann heard the distinct mental click that told her once again, Caro was right.

"So, what do you think?"

"I think healing takes time. And Jason will still have some problems to face. But readers will know that he'll get through them. Not so much because of Heather's love and support, which he'll always have. But because she's opened him up to accepting his emotions without always judging and beating himself up over them."

"So, you're okay with that?"

"Absolutely." More than okay. Once again, Caro had come through. In fact, Meghann was already looking forward to writing Jason's three-tissue good-bye scene with his gramps. "Thanks."

"Just doing my job. Thank *you* for making me look so good these past years. Not to mention the year-end bonuses that buy more shoes than anyone but Carrie Bradshaw should actually own. And you don't have to remind me that she was fictional. I can tell the difference. At least most of the time." She lifted her glass. "To great sales and yet more new readers joining your legion of fans."

They toasted, then admired the beautifully plated lunch the waiter placed on the table with appropriate ceremony.

"I do have something else to tell you," Caro said.

"Oh?" Meghann took a bite of pasta and

nearly swooned as the browned butter and sage sauce contrasted perfectly with the sweetness of the pumpkin.

"You received an email."

"And that's unusual why?" Because she'd learned early on how enthusiastic her young audience could be, after wearing out two assistants in a six-month period, Meghann had had taken Caro's advice and had all mail sent directly to her publisher.

"This one's for a fundraiser."

"Again, not unusual." Another thing she'd learned early on in her career was how many groups there were out there in the world raising money for various causes. And although she did her best, she'd also had to accept that she couldn't save the entire world single-handedly.

"True. But the guy who wrote the letter says he used to know you."

Meghann put down her fork. "Okay, I'll bite. Who?"

"Adam Wayne. In Shelter Bay, Oregon. Which is where you grew up, right?"

Adam? Seriously? And how was it that just hearing his name caused her unruly heart to skip a beat?

"I moved around a lot." Major understatement there. "But I did go through high school in Shelter Bay." While living in three different foster homes, but hey, who was counting? Meghann had long ago accepted that she continued to live those years, which were both the best and worst of times, through her semi-autobiographical teen novels.

"It took a while to reach me because you keep the mail room busy and we have a couple of layers of interns culling out the more personal things to send to me." She reached down into an alligator bag the size of Texas, pulled out the folded printout, and handed it across the table.

Just seeing his name after all these years caused Meghann to be bombarded by so many emotions she wouldn't be surprised if her body was emitting flashing lights as bright as the ones wrapped around the restaurant's pillars.

"So you *do* know him?"

"I do. Did." She skimmed the single page, noting with some measure of pride that Adam had remembered his punctuation rules.

"From the way your face lit up, then turned the color of your martini, I sense a story."

"I tutored Adam our senior year."

"Ah, he was one of those jocks you wrote all the book reports for." *The ones who never asked you out*, Meghann knew Caro was thinking but did not say.

"No. Adam was a science nerd whose IQ was off the charts. But for some reason, except for science fiction and fantasy genres, he couldn't get his mind wrapped around the classics that were being taught in class. And while he could probably program Java in his sleep, his punctuation skills were nonexistent. Which was a problem because, although everyone else had pretty much let him slide through because of his mad ninja genius skills, his senior-year English teacher refused to allow anyone to leave his class without an ability to express thoughts in writing. All the blue marks on his essays had knocked his grade down to a D minus. Which was dragging his GPA down into the danger zone when I was brought in."

"So, since you were the class bookworm, you were recruited?"

"Pretty much. Although my senior year foster parents insisted on giving me what the state gave them for my care, every dollar helped, so I picked up some extra money tutoring on the side."

She left unsaid that by the time the first hour lesson was over, Meghann would have tutored Adam Wayne for free. "I also was in charge of the library at a summer camp for separated foster kids, but that was volunteer."

"I'd guess the situation must have hit close to home."

"You'd guess right. I'm not going to lie and say that it was easy being a foster kid, but I couldn't imagine what it must be like to have families broken up and siblings sent to different homes." The nonprofit camp had allowed children to reunite for two weeks each year. "Adam ran the science workshops."

"Ah." Caro tilted her head and studied Meghann as she took a sip of her martini. "Another story? A camp counselor romance?"

"No. Not really."

That one summer night, when Adam, now Dr. Adam Wayne, Ph.D., had given Meghann her first kiss couldn't really count as even a short story. Except for the fact that it had been better than she'd ever imagined any kiss could be. Even superior to those romances she'd checked out from the bookmobile that had arrived in Shelter

Bay every two weeks before the branch library had been built. There'd been more stolen kisses, but by Labor Day Meghann had learned the hard way that summer romances were a lot like sandcastles, predestined to crumble and wash away.

"So now the boy genius has returned to his hometown to open a hands-on science museum for local kids."

"Apparently so." Adam had written asking for a donation of books for a fundraiser. Which made sense since she was undoubtedly on the donator list for the construction of the library.

"I suppose you want me to take care of having some of the autographed copies we keep on hand sent out?" Caro said.

"No." While she hadn't seen or heard from Adam for ages, the request was personal enough that Meghann wanted to handle it herself. "Since there's a phone number with his signature, I'll give him a call myself after lunch. By that time he should be at work." Both the contact email address and phone number below his signature belonged to Coastal Community College in Shelter Bay.

Apparently sometime after grad school at

2

ADAM WAYNE'S DAY was not starting out on a high note. After spending half the night out on a boat in an icy December rain, bucking choppy Pacific waves looking for a solitary whale that had been reported breaching off the coast, he was in serious need of coffee.

Which wouldn't be a problem if only sometime in the past week he'd remembered to buy any.

Which he hadn't.

Making matters worse was the power outage that had occurred sometime after four a.m. when he arrived home, which meant his bedside clock radio alarm hadn't gone off at six thirty. His backup cell alarm had probably rung, but unfortunately he'd left the phone in the inside pocket of his parka hanging on a hook in the mudroom. It was undoubtedly still set on vibrate, which he used when he didn't want his class lectures interrupted.

After whipping through a glacial, thirty-second sailor shower because he couldn't take the time for the ancient, rattling water heater to warm up, he tossed on some clothes, stuffed the exam papers he'd managed to grade before going out on the *Sea Wolf* into his backpack, and while keeping to the speed limit—because Sheriff Kara Douchett was a stickler for law and order—headed up Harborview, then up the hills, and past the stone statue of the fisherman's wife, who eternally awaited her husband's return home from the sea. Someone had decked her out with a Christmas crown of candles atop her bronze head in an homage to all the Swedish loggers and fishermen who'd helped settle Shelter Bay.

Coastal Community College was set up on a bluff high on a hill overlooking the harbor. While admittedly not the largest nor the most prestigious school in the state, it suited Adam just fine. After two undergraduate years at Cal-Poly before transferring to Duke's marine science program, he'd been lured back to the Pacific Northwest by an offer to establish a whale research program funded by a gazillionaire tech mogul who cared as much about the ancient mammals as Adam, himself did. With his hometown's pod of resident whales and Oregon State University's Hatfield Marine Science Center just down the coast in Newport, Shelter Bay had been a logical place to set up shop. Meanwhile, his two classes at the local college allowed him to satisfy his love of teaching while giving him time for research. A definite win/win.

He pulled up into the parking lot surrounded by towering fir trees and entered the lighthouse-white science building with its red-tile roof five minutes before his first class was to begin. Which gave him just enough time to duck into the administration office.

"You're out of coffee again," Dee Kentta, the woman behind the desk guessed. Although her job description might technically be administrative assistant, the grandmother of five was more the admiral who ran the science department ship.

Which wasn't easy, Adam allowed, given that the stereotype about absent-minded scientists wasn't entirely off the mark. An avid knitter in the Coastal Salishan tradition, she'd not only made everyone in the department scarves for

Christmas, she was a walking gallery of her work. Today's red sweater bore a stylized black, brown, white, and red Native American salmon design.

"Guilty."

"I'm going to request administration get me one of those Keurig machines," she complained as she bustled over to the table that held a hot plate and two carafes. "That way, all you absent-minded geniuses can just put in one of those little pods, press the button, and get your own drink instead of making me get up and down all day."

"I love you," he said happily as steam wafted up from the cardboard cup of Cape Foulweather's Drifter's Blend roast she handed him. "I don't suppose you'd marry me and let me take you away from all this?"

She planted her hands on her hips. "You just want to get my coffee all to yourself."

"That, too. But I also have mad crazy love for your organizational skills and the fact that you're an exotically beautiful woman who always smells like cinnamon rolls." He leaned across the counter and sniffed appreciatively.

"Go away with you, Dr. Wayne," she complained with a laugh. Then turned serious. "Did you hear about the whale?"

"Yeah."

"So what are you going to do about it?"

And hadn't he asked himself that for most of the night? "I can't do anything if I can't find him. If he even exists. It's not as if there aren't a lot of whales out there this time of year. And besides, the water was so choppy, it could've just been a log."

"No one around here's going to mistake a killer whale for a log," she scoffed.

Which was mostly true Adam allowed. This time of year, as the migration occurred, whales were a common sight off shore. While boats made a good living taking tourists out to view the whales, most locals, accustomed to their own pod, no longer considered the towering plume of exhaled water or a breaching exotic. Which didn't mean that even the most jaded failed to find the sight amazing. Whales were so much a part of the ocean landscape that even many school children could recognize the migrating mammals by the shape and markings of their dorsal fins. Many people kept journals of migrating whales, knowing them by official tagged numbers or more familiarly by names given to them over the years.

"It's been foggy. And rainy." Surprise surprise. What would have been unusual this time of year was if the sea *hadn't* been draped in rain, fog, and low-hanging thick pewter clouds.

"Some are saying it's the captain," Dee said. "Even during his busiest season, he'd try to get home for the solstice celebration. It only makes sense he'd want to comfort his family this year."

The captain was Joe Bayaa, whose fishing boat, *The Salishan*, had gone down in a storm last month in Bristol Bay while crabbing. As the boats had decks loaded with seven-hundred-pound crab pots, it was surprising that more didn't capsize. There was a reason the TV show had been called *The Deadliest Catch*.

Adam also knew that despite being a woman of the twenty-first century, Dee managed to bridge modern life with the time of her ancestors, embracing many traditional aspects of her culture. Including the taboo of naming the dead, thus the use of Joe's nickname, rather than his birth name.

Adam also knew that coastal Native Americans considered the Orca to be the wolf's counterpart in the ocean, which put it at the top of their animal hierarchy. A position Joe had held in tribal life, as well.

"One thing working with whales has taught me is that just when you think you've got them all figured out, they'll surprise you," he said. As a scientist, Adam believed in facts. But just as he couldn't prove whales were spirit animals, there was no way to disprove the ancient belief, either. So he remained basically agnostic on the topic.

"It's him," Dee repeated. "His spirit was definitely in the house last night. Everyone there felt him." She glanced up at the large wall clock. "So there's no reason to argue the point. Especially when you're going to be late to class. *Again.*"

"Yes, Mom." He flashed her his best grin, which only had her shaking her dark head in what he knew was mock frustration.

After walking down a hallway lined with Native American art that echoed that on Dee's sweater, Adam was nearly to the door of his classroom when his phone vibrated. The screen showed a name that was a decided blast from his past.

After three months, he'd given up waiting for Meghann to respond to his email. What had he expected? His former tutor and fellow high school nerd was no longer that pretty girl who spent lunches sitting beneath a tree or at a table at the far end of the cafeteria, her cute little upturned nose stuck in a book.

Now she wrote books hundreds of thousands of teenagers and even many adults read. Including, he'd noticed, his own students. Her chatty YouTube videos were an internet sensation, and from what he'd read in the *Shelter Bay Beacon*, there was talk of a major movie deal in the works.

Hell, he'd told himself after three weeks had gone by, she probably didn't even remember him. It wasn't as if he'd been hot, like those jocks whose book reports she was always writing. He'd worn glasses for his nearsightedness before Johnny Depp and Brad Pitt had made them cool and carried a briefcase—kill me now, he thought with an inner cringe at the memory—crammed with books by Hubble, Hawking, and Sagan. That had been back in his astronomy days, before two weeks at Camp Rainbow with geography and ecology professor Fred Dalton had changed not only his view of the world but his life.

Realizing that if he stared at the screen any longer, her call would go into voice mail, he swiped the slider with enough force to bobble the coffee, which, despite the biodegradable plastic top Dee had put on it, sloshed over his hand and down the front of his jeans.

"Damn!" Making a quick decision, he dropped the phone instead of the coffee. His junk was on fire, but even he knew you didn't grab your crotch in the hallway outside a classroom filled with eighteen-to-twenty-year-olds.

One he'd gotten a handle on the cup, thus allowing for possible future generations of Waynes, he scooped the phone from the floor.

"Uh…hi," he said. Great opening line, numbnuts.

"Adam?" All these years later, and her voice was as familiar as his own. Which wasn't exactly all that surprising, given that he'd been hearing it in his dreams for the past three months ever since high school physics teacher, basketball coach, and hoops buddy Dillon Slater had pushed him into contacting her.

"Yeah. It's me. Meghann?"

"You recognized me?" She sounded as surprised as he'd been to hear from her. Then, before he could respond, she said, "Duh." He could practically envision her slapping her forehead. "Caller ID."

"Yeah…" A pause began to stretch out. Not that it was awkward or anything. "I didn't expect to hear from you."

"I'm sorry." She sounded sincere. "I tried to call you after I finally got your email yesterday, but I guess you were out."

"Yeah. I was." And damn, he'd been so wiped out when he'd gotten home, he'd forgotten to check for messages. And this morning had been too hectic. "I'm sorry I didn't get your message. And you don't have to apologize. You undoubtedly get a lot of mail for your people to wade through."

"My readership demographic is very vocal," she agreed. "Which is why, if I read all my mail myself, I'd never get any books written."

"In which case you wouldn't have to worry about reader mail. Because you wouldn't have any. Which becomes a classic case of temporal causality loop."

"Like *Groundhog Day*."

"Got it in one. It also happened in the season five 'Cause and Effect' episode of *Star Trek:*

The Next Generation."

"I missed that one." He wasn't surprised. She'd never been a fan of the genre, though she had once admitted a secret crush on Mr. Spock. "In the beginning of my career, I answered all my mail. I miss that feedback."

Adam thought he heard a sigh. Which brought back that rainy April day in his bedroom when, as a joke, he'd had a *Heathcliff was a Douche* T-shirt printed at a shop on Harborview, and wore it to their tutoring session. While struggling to explain the concept of an anti-hero—which, thank you, having reached epic level in Dungeons & Dragons before he'd gotten out of middle school, he was well acquainted with, it was just jerks raised up as romantic icons he had a problem with—she'd exhaled a long, frustrated sigh.

They'd been face-to-face, so close he could see her eyes glitter like green dragon scales beneath a mega sun as they'd argued about the fictional guy who'd not only be considered a douche by today's standards, but probably a psychopath. Meghann had been so close that her breath had felt like a warm, minty breeze against his neck, which, despite what he'd learned in anatomy class, had become directly connected to his penis.

Adam had always had a better than average memory, which was why that moment over a decade ago, was frozen in amber, like dinosaur DNA from *Jurassic Park*.

As a slideshow of the flare of heat in her re- markably expressive eyes appeared in HD on an IMAX screen in his mind, his body responded exactly as it had that long-ago day. Unfortunate- ly, while his autobiographical memory might be stellar, his hearing apparently didn't work all that well during a sexual brain fog. Belatedly realizing she'd said something, he was able to rewind and pull her words back up.

"I hope I'm not too late to contribute," she'd said.

"Not at all," he assured her. "We had an ini- tial fundraiser in October, which was the one I wrote to you about. But there's going to be a silent auction at the Snow Ball on New Year's Eve. If you'd like to donate some books for that—"

"Absolutely. In fact, what would you say to me auctioning off the opportunity to have a character named after the winner in my next book?"

"That would be great. And would probably pay for our tactile dome. Maybe even the lightning show that was planned for much further in the future."

"Oh, that sounds like so much fun! Is the auction listed online?"

"It's on Shelter Bay's Facebook page."

"Terrific," she said after he'd given her the URL. "I'll post the news of the fundraiser on Facebook, Twitter, Pinterest, Instagram, and YouTube this afternoon."

"You'd do all that?"

"Of course. It'll be such a great thing for the kids. From your email sig line, I take it you're teaching at CCC?"

She sounded a bit surprised by that. A few years ago, he would've been too. "A couple courses. Mostly I'm doing research on the nighttime diving behavior of various species of whales. Which makes Shelter Bay ideal, thanks to our resident population and its location in the migratory path. We've been getting around fifty new whales a day."

"I envy you. I read in the *Times* that we had a record number of Humpbacks here on the East

Coast last winter, but I was so deep in deadline hell I barely got out of my apartment, let alone to the shore to watch them."

"Too bad."

"I thought so at the time. I've admittedly lost touch with everyone from my Shelter Bay days and hadn't realized that you'd switched to whale research."

"That was thanks to Fred Dalton. Those classes he taught at Camp Rainbow encouraged me to stop looking up at the stars and start observing the world around me." By teaching, Adam liked to think he was following in Fred's footsteps.

"Nothing wrong with stargazing," she said.

Adam couldn't argue with that, since it had been a way to get Meghann away from the others at night and impress her with his knowledge of astronomy. Later he'd come to realize that explaining all about the sequence of the planets and naming various stars hadn't exactly been the coolest of make-out moves.

"True. But after two years of astrophysics, I switched to marine biology. Which is how I eventually ended up back here. Thanks to you."

"Me?"

"Without your tutoring, I never would've been able to write those important essays when I applied to Cal-Poly. And no way could I have filled out all those grant proposals, which eventually landed me my dream gig."

"That's sweet of you to say."

"It's the truth." Even though he would've enjoyed talking to her for hours, he glanced into the window of his classroom. Unlike the chaos his absence might have caused at the high school where Dillon taught physics, Adam's students had so far remained in their seats. *So far* being the definitive words.

"I just turned in a manuscript," she said.

"That's going to make a lot of readers happy."

"One can hope. What if I came out there?"

"Here? To Shelter Bay?" Adam's only excuse for the lame questions was that Meghann had always been able to fog his mind. From that first moment she'd walked into homeroom, a transfer student from Seattle, a mass of curly red hair tumbling over her shoulders and gleaming like the sun setting into the sea, Adam had known what it must feel like to see the aurora borealis for the very first time.

"My best friend just decided to go to Connecticut for Christmas," Meghann said. "The past few years we've spent Christmas binge-watching holiday movies and eating take-out Chinese, so I hadn't made any other plans. So, since it was looking as if I'd have to spend the holiday with General Tso, I'd rather come watch whales and see if I can help raise more money."

Was she saying she wanted to come watch whales with him? Damn. Despite having scored a perfect SAT score, thanks again in part to her tutoring, he still had trouble with the vague nuances women littered throughout their conversations. He'd often thought pulling off cold fusion would be a snap compared to decoding the female mind.

"It gets awfully cold out on the water this time of year," he warned.

"It's winter," she reminded him. "It gets really cold in New York this time of year too."

Was she laughing at him? Adam could practically see that dancing glint she'd get in her eyes whenever she'd teased him. They both might have been nerds, but Meghann had been light years ahead of him in social skills. Which had served her well in all those YouTube videos he'd spent too many late nights watching the past few months since writing that letter.

"There's an early flight out of La Guardia tomorrow morning," she said. "If I don't get stranded in Denver because of a blizzard, I could be in Portland by noon. Then, taking time to rent a car—"

"I'll pick you up."

"That's not necessary."

"The coastal mountains can be dangerous this time of year with all those grades and curves and black ice even for a driver who isn't out of practice." A bus carrying the Shelter Bay Ski Club had crashed just a couple years ago.

"What makes you think I'm out of practice?"

"Do you own a car?"

"No. That'd be impractical in the city. But they do have car rentals in New York."

"When was the last time you drove?"

She hesitated. "Two years ago," she conceded. "But I'll still need a car while I'm in town."

"No problem. As it happens, I've got two vehicles. The guy who funds my whale research showed up with one for me last month and between the night research, my classes, and the fund-raising, I've been too busy to list my SUV for sale. You can use it for as long as you want."

"That's very generous."

"You're the one who's going to be bringing in big bucks for the museum," he pointed out. "Seems like giving you wheels while you're here is the least I can do."

"Well, I'm grateful. Since the only thing the rental place had left was a compact, which honestly concerned me."

"You've already checked."

It was not a question, but she answered it anyway. "Yesterday afternoon. When I booked what appeared to be the last ticket out of New York. It's a middle seat in the back row, but you've no idea how much I'm looking forward to being back in Shelter Bay."

Not nearly as much as he was looking forward to having her back in town. After she gave him her flight number and times, Adam ended the call.

Then before going into his classroom, he pumped the fist holding the phone in the air.

3

"YOU NEVER SAID you knew Meghann Quinn personally," Dillon Slater said as he and Adam sat at the bar at Bon Temps, a Cajun restaurant and dance hall, scarfing down oyster po' boys. Adam had just related his earlier phone call.

"It's a small town. You know how it is. Everyone in school pretty much knew everyone else. Besides, it wasn't important." Adam dunked a French fry into a dish of the restaurant's signature spicy red "come back" sauce.

"Yet you emailed her without having mentioned anything about it."

"You suggested I write because we'd been in the same graduating class. I didn't bring up having been friends because I didn't want to get everyone's hopes up. When I sent the request for autographed books for the fundraiser to her publisher I had no idea it'd even get to her."

"If you were friends, why didn't you just write her? Why go through her publisher?"

"I didn't have any contact information."

Dillon lifted a brow. "Like you couldn't hack into the publisher's system and retrieve it with both hands tied behind your back," he said. "Hell, I don't have half your mad computer powers and I could probably pull it off."

"And geez, wouldn't that be an excellent role model for the kids we're trying to inspire?" Adam asked dryly. "Besides, I prefer to use my superpowers for good."

"There's also the fact that my wife would have to arrest you," Sax Douchett, a former Navy SEAL and owner of Bon Temps said as he washed glasses in the bar sink. Not only was Kara Douchett Shelter Bay's sheriff, local gossip had Sax having been secretly in love with her back when they'd been kids and she'd only had eyes for his best friend. Who'd later tragically been killed after surviving two tours in Iraq.

"There is that," Adam agreed. Not that crime was a major problem in this small coastal town—though there were stories of a couple of more recent incidences that would have made good Dateline *Real Mystery* episodes—but the sheriff, a former Shelter Bay High School valedictorian a few years ahead of Adam, remained ever vigilant.

He crunched through the cornmeal and panko breading on the deep-fried oyster and decided if heaven actually existed and had a taste, Bon Temps' po' boys could well come close. "And speaking of your pistol-packing wife, can I ask you a question?"

"Shoot."

"How did you move Kara from the friend zone to getting her to agree to marry you?"

"Well, there were a few steps in between," Sax said. "But the key was that although it wasn't easy staying patient, especially when I wanted to jump her every chance I got, I took things slow." His smile was obnoxiously satisfied. "Still do, most of the time. Except when I don't."

"Damn. TMI, Douchett," Dillon complained as he jabbed a fry into the red sauce.

"Hey." Sax shrugged. "Don't blame me. Mr. Peabody here is the one who asked." He picked up a towel and began drying a pilsner glass. "You got someone in mind who has you asking? Like that hot writer you're not willing to risk jail time for?"

Adam shrugged. "I didn't say anything about her being hot."

"I didn't know Meghann Quinn back in the day, being that I'd already left town when her family arrived, but I saw her latest in a window display at Tidal Wave Books. Even if I didn't have a thing for redheads, having married one myself, the woman would definitely classify as hot."

"Between magma and the center of a black hole," Dillon agreed.

Adam knew he was entering a danger zone when a spark of jealousy flared. "You guys are married."

"Happily," Sax agreed.

"Deliriously," Dillon echoed. He took a swig of Captain Sig's Northwestern Ale, wiping the foam off his mouth with the back of his hand. "But for the record, marriage doesn't turn a guy blind. I've been looking at that woman's photo on the back of books ever since I started teaching. Seems every girl in school, and not a few guys, are carrying them around. She's totally a fox."

"She's a nice woman." Granted, he hadn't seen Meghann in person in over a decade, but she'd been a really smart, nice girl, and from their phone conversation, fame and the fast pace of New York life hadn't changed her.

Dillon's dark brows climbed his forehead. "Did I say she wasn't?"

"Sounds as if he's a little sensitive where the lady's concerned," Sax offered.

"No. I'm not. And did you learn that damn look from your cop wife?" he shot back as Sax gave him a straight-on, slitted-eye stare.

"No. I developed it all on my own, while trying to decide whether or not some goat farmer in Afghanistan was going to blow me up or take me prisoner," the other man, who for a time had been held captive in an enemy village, countered.

"Fine. Play the damn war card," Adam muttered.

"Just saying," Sax said as he began dusting the higher-priced bottles on the top shelf, which didn't get a lot of orders.

"There's something I don't understand," Dillon said.

"What now?" Adam wasn't used to having his personal life dissected. Maybe because, up until now, he hadn't really had anything resembling a personal life.

"The autographed books will bring in some donations. And having her do that name-a-character thing, especially putting it out there on social media, should score big bucks. But she doesn't need to come here to do that."

"So?" Adam could hear the question coming and didn't want to admit he'd been wondering the same thing.

"So, why is she coming all the way across the country during the worst travel week of the year?"

"Maybe because she felt like it. Plus, she told me she didn't have anything else to do."

"Yeah. I can imagine finding something to do in New York City would be a real challenge," Sax said over his shoulder.

It was Adam's turn to take a long drink of his Dead Guy Ale. "Hell, I don't know. I'm not her damn social secretary."

"You should take her to the Snow Ball," Sax suggested. Having finished his dusting, he began hanging the newly washed glasses in their rack.

"Yeah," Dillon piled on. "Her being there will draw more people to the silent auction."

"Not to mention the fact that the *Shelter Bay Beacon* will write a story with photos, which could get picked up by search engines and gain more attention to your museum," Sax said.

"You do realize that the appeal of a small town might be to avoid things like balls and getting your picture in the paper." Adam would throw himself off the Shelter Bay drawbridge before admitting that the fantasy of taking Meghann Quinn to the Snow Ball had gone through his mind. Okay, he wouldn't lie. It had also stuck there. "She's a writer, not some movie star or socialite who thrives on publicity."

She'd also been shy back in high school and just because she'd appeared chatty and engaging on those videos didn't necessarily mean that wasn't an alter ego she'd taken on for her audience. Adam knew a lot about pretending to be someone you weren't.

Back in the day when he'd had to go begging for grant money for his study, he'd put on the charcoal-gray suit and white dress shirt his sister, Jill, had made him buy. He'd ended up having to buy a second after he'd left the room to add something to his PowerPoint presentation and returned to a rust-brown imprint in the shape of an iron on the shirt's front. And thanks to the same YouTube that had made Meghann an

Internet star, he'd learned to tie a half Windsor knot in the yellow tie Jill had assured him was a power color.

Then, decked out in the business equivalent of Tony Stark's Iron Man suit, he'd go out into the world, trying to convince billionaire captains of industry on the idea that saving endangered whales might possibly earn them some karma points to help make up for having endangered the world's largest and most intelligent mammals in the first place.

Not that he'd added that last part. But he'd definitely thought it.

Ultimately, proving the Henry David Thoreau axiom about not needing new suits for new ventures (which he'd first learned when Meghann had made him read *Walden*), he'd gotten a seemingly unlimited grant from a thirty-something gazillionaire tech mogul who'd been comfortably and, to Adam's mind, *sensibly* dressed in faded jeans, an open-necked plaid shirt and well-worn Nikes.

"If you ask her to the Snow Ball you'll get to dance with her," Sax pointed out.

"And maybe get lucky afterwards," Dillon said in a reminiscent way that suggested he had personal experience in that area. "And don't even try to claim you weren't thinking along those lines when you first wrote that email."

"It might have crossed my mind... Okay," he said at Sax's knowing snort. "If only I only had a DeLorean, I'd go back in time and change a lot of things. Like letting her go off to college at Columbia without telling her how I felt about her."

"Now we're getting somewhere. Which allows me to return home since I know Claire's going to grill me for details," Dillon said. Having finished his lunch, he scooped up a handful of bar nuts. "How *did* you feel about her?"

"It was complicated. We were both only eighteen." And virgins, but some details didn't need sharing.

"An age when guys are thinking more with their little heads than their big ones," said Sax, whose reputation with women was Shelter Bay legend. That was before Kara had managed to mostly settle the former bad boy SEAL down, making Adam wonder if she kept a lion tamer's whip and a chair up in their oceanfront house.

"It wasn't like that," he said. "Okay, hell,

maybe it was, but having sex back then wouldn't have been logical."

Dillon spit out the drink of ale he'd just taken to cool the flames from the infamously fiery nuts. "Holy shit. You actually used logical and sex in the same sentence. Next you'll tell us you're from the planet Vulcan."

"We were kids. I was going to school in California and she was off to New York—"

"And they didn't have planes back then?"

"Sure. But we had life plans all mapped out. Do you have any idea how many people's lives get screwed up because a girl gets pregnant and they get married too young?"

"I haven't a clue," Sax said. "And even if I did, I'd feel the need to point out that Kara married Jared right after high school and if he hadn't gotten killed on a damn domestic violence call, they probably would've made it."

Which would've meant there never would've been a Sax and Kara. As a scientist, Adam had never believed in fate or destiny. But more and more, as a man, looking at two friends whose twisting personal roads had led them to the women they were obviously meant to be with, and especially when his mind drifted to a certain woman with emerald eyes and hair the bright and shining color of a setting sun, Adam sometimes wondered.

4

AS IF FATE, Mother Nature, or the airline gods had conspired to be on her side, Meghann's flight proved uneventful. She even lucked out when whoever was supposed to be sitting in the window seat had either missed his or her flight or just didn't show up. Which allowed her to claim it, leaving an empty seat between her and a seemingly mute teenager who was content to isolate himself with headphones while playing a video game.

Because she'd lived in the east so many years, where the mountains had been worn down by age, the view along the Columbia River Gorge as the plane approached Portland took her breath away. Moments later, she was looking directly into the snow-topped summit of Mt. Hood, with Mt. Adams appearing equally close on the other side of the plane. Right before they descended into a cloudbank, she also caught a glimpse of

Mt. St. Helens, with its lopsided top due to that eruption in the '80s, and in the distance, the towering Mt. Rainier.

Despite being crowded with holiday travelers, the terminal still managed to lack the manic stress-producing energy usually attributed to airports. Once again, Portland, Oregon was living up to its mellow, laid-back reputation.

She made her way past the restaurants and shops, all decorated for the season, to the baggage claim at the lower level where she and Adam had agreed to meet.

The moment she saw him, looking so much like the boy she'd once been in love with but still so different, Meghann's heart stopped. As did her feet, which seemed to be glued to the floor.

But she must have been the only one of them uncomfortable because his bearded face lit up with a smile and his gray eyes, which had once been nearly covered by a thick fringe of bangs due more to not getting regular haircuts than any fashion statement, warmed to the color of burnished pewter.

Instructing her feet to move again, she walked toward him as he walked toward her. "Hi," she said when they met in the middle.

"Hi, yourself." His eyes crinkled as he grinned down at her.

Having gone through a growing spurt that summer of her tailor-made-for-the-Lifetime-channel teen romance, Adam had been tall and painfully skinny, which had had the boy campers tagging him with the name Jack Skellington, the skeleton character from *The Nightmare Before Christmas.*

The girls apparently were more discriminating, since most of them had harbored crushes on the teenage science instructor. He'd filled out during the intervening years, possessing the rangy, lean-muscled body of a long-distance runner.

"You look great," he said.

She ran a hand over her hair, which she could feel springing into Little Orphan Annie corkscrews. The constant opening and closing of the automatic doors leading outside was bringing in the humidity from the winter drizzle falling outside.

Remembering what she'd told her sixteen-year-old self on that first YouTube video she'd done at the urging of her publisher, she refrained from pointing out that the expensive frizz fighter potion she bought in bulk was having a total smoothing fail moment. Instead, she smiled back up at him. "So do you. I like your hair."

Unlike hers, his was behaving, rocking a Jake Gyllenhaal spiked up bedhead. Which took her mind to a place it really didn't need to go.

Shaking off the vision of Adam Wayne climbing out of bed (Would he wear boxers? Briefs? Nothing at all?) she said, "It's been a long time." Talk about stating the obvious. Even the most socially inept of her characters were better conversationalists.

"Too long," he agreed.

Then, putting his hand on her back, he guided her through the throng of travelers toward the luggage carousel. His light touch felt both protective and a bit possessive, which should have irked. She'd come a long way from that shy wallflower she'd once been. She was a New York woman who didn't need a man to physically direct her through traffic as if she were some frail flower that might get her delicate petals trampled. But since she didn't want to start things off with negative behavior, and because, damn it, his hand felt so good against the back of her jacket, she didn't pull away.

They managed to make small talk as they waited for her luggage. About her flight, the meal, that was no longer served in coach—but hey, she could buy some sunflower seeds—and the wonder of flying over the Rockies and Cascades, which had made the lack of any meals worthwhile. He caught her up on the fundraiser and she told him how good it felt, after the past months spent deep in Fictionland, to rejoin the real world.

Adam did not say how much he liked the way her ivory sweater, which was woven from some fluffy material that reminded him of clouds, hugged her breasts beneath that open yellow rain parka. Nor did he add that as pretty as she looked in it, he wouldn't mind lowering that metal zipper running down the front.

And even as he could hear Sax and Dillon ragging him, he didn't ask her to the Snow Ball.

She didn't say how she'd been hit by that un-expected lightning bolt of lust the moment she'd seen him. Nor how his touch had brought back last night's too-vivid dream where that hand he'd placed so casually on her back had created havoc over every inch of her needy, neglected body.

And, although she knew that Caro would

never have been so tongue-tied, Meghann couldn't figure out a way to ask him if he was taking anyone to the Snow Ball. And if not, would he take her?

It was, she thought with a long, inward sigh, just like high school all over again.

"That's mine," she said, pointing out the bag as it rumbled toward them.

"Got it." He leaned forward, scooped it up and put it down beside them. "How many more?"

"That's it." She could tell by the way his brow lifted that surprised him. "What, were you expecting a flotilla of alligator bags with fancy designer logos?"

"I hadn't exactly narrowed it down to those details. Especially since I don't think I own two pieces of luggage that match. But, although, as a biologist, I'm grateful anytime someone opts for cloth instead of gator, yeah, I figured you'd have more."

"You learn to travel light on book tours," she said. "If it were summer, I'd have a smaller bag. And I usually carry on, but this time they were stopping everyone at the gate and checking everyone's bags."

"My mom used to take a separate case just for shoes if we were going away for a weekend," he said.

"I'm not your mother." For this trip to rainy Oregon, she'd opted for a practical pair of low-heeled black rain boots that ended at mid calf.

"Thank God," she thought she heard him mutter, but the loud announcement of an arriving flight kept her from being sure.

This past August Caro had taken a suitcase nearly the size of a steamer trunk to spend a weekend at the Hamptons. Which was totally alien behavior to Meghann. Although she could describe with detail what every character in any of Jane Austen's books wore and always kept up with teenage fashions in order to dress her characters, when it came to buying her own clothes, she was as clueless as she'd been back when she'd been forced to shop at thrift stores.

Finally they were in the car, headed toward the coast. As if to fill the silence stretching between them, he hit a button on the SUV's steering wheel, turning on the radio.

"Sorry," he said as Trisha Yearwood's "Never Let You Go Again" started playing. He reached over to change stations. "You probably don't like this stuff anymore."

"I write stories," she said mildly. "Country songs tell stories." And didn't this particular one hit home? Another thing she hadn't told Adam was that his email had gotten her wondering about second chances. "Why wouldn't I like still like them?"

"You've been away a long time."

"True. As were you. Before you came back."

"I wasn't in New York City."

"Again, true. But believe it or not, New York isn't on a different planet. Not only does it have barbecue, it also has a country music station." Okay, maybe only one these days, but still...

This conversation, coming right after his suitcase remarks, had her wondering if he believed she could have actually changed so much. Which in turn made her wonder if he'd known her at all back then.

Which was beyond depressing.

"It's really great of you to come," he said.

"I'm happy to. As I said, you're saving me from spending the next few days binge watching *A Wonderful Life*, *Love Actually*, *The Holiday*, *While You Were Sleeping*, and *Die Hard*.

"That last one is a surprise for someone who

used to be a romantic."

"I still am." Unfortunately. "And *Die Hard* is romantic. Really," she insisted as he shot her a skeptical look. "It's obvious John McClane still loves his wife and wants to reconcile, but being a stereotypical tough, silent alpha guy, he can't come up with the words to tell her. But then Alan Rickman arrives with his bad guys and takes her hostage, which gives him a chance to prove his love by saving her."

"With a lot of gunfire and explosions."

"Which could have been meant metaphorically but were probably thrown in to get guys into the seats."

Adam couldn't argue with that. Especially since even in nerdland he couldn't imagine many guys who would blast love songs on a boom box outside a girl's bedroom window or sing to her from the bleachers like those DVDs he remembered Meghann watching in the counselor's lounge at Camp Rainbow. Just because Cusak and Ledger had been able to pull off those stunts, didn't mean an average guy could.

"A lot of guys probably fantasize, at least sometime in their lives, winning the girl in some kind of battle," he said. Another reason for the popularity of the Star Wars franchise. Unfortunately, most of the guys he'd hung with back in high school had been like him—unlikely to ever be mistaken for Han Solo.

"Which is why the Willis character works for both genders." Meghann was proving as earnest as back when she'd been trying to explain the romantic appeal of Heathcliff and Mr. Darcy. Who, for the record, didn't, in any way Adam could see, share any traits with Willis's John McClane. Proving yet again the mysterious dichotomy of female minds. "He doesn't back down and he never gives up. He just keeps killing the bad guys."

"The guy in *The Notebook* wrote three hundred and sixty-five letters. McClane writes notes on the sweatshirts of dead terrorists and throws them out the window. That's how he communicates love?"

"It's not exactly like *The Notebook*, where Noah wrote all those letters to Allie," Meghann allowed. "But love is situational. In New York a man might show feelings for a woman by snagging a taxi for her at rush hour. And I'll admit to being surprised you watched that movie."

"Jill insisted on downloading it the last time she visited with the kids from Portland. Despite all the years of social work, somehow she still looks at the world through rose-colored glasses."

"I think that's a wonderful attitude for the people she's helping. There were times a caring social worker made a big difference in my life."

Although Meghann hadn't shared all the details of her life with him, given that she was constantly moving from home to home, life hadn't been easy. Which, he suspected, contributed to her success. He'd read her books—at first out of curiosity and later because he recognized so much of his own high school life in the stories—and had been impressed by how she'd managed to inject serious topics with such a deft and light touch.

His phone buzzed. Adam hit the little icon on the steering wheel. "Hey."

"You've got a floatplane," the familiar voice of his research's benefactor coming out of the dashboard speaker informed him. "The pilot's waiting for you at the harbor. The rain's stopped off the coast so you should have clear skies this afternoon."

Damn. The good news was that the floatplane would help expand his search for the supposedly lost Orca. The bad news was that he'd been hoping to spend some personal time alone with Meghann before having to share her with the rest of Shelter Bay.

"Tell the pilot to go have himself some lunch, and I'll be there in a couple hours," he said.

"Roger that."

"You're leaving town?" Meghann asked as Adam ended the call. Was that disappointment he heard in her voice?

"No. I'm just looking for a migrating Orca who might have gotten himself separated from his pod. I've been out the past couple of nights on my boat, but the fog hangs low to the water at night, so I couldn't see anything. I was hoping a plane would expand the search."

"What will you do if you do find it?"

"Good question... Want to come with me?"

"Seriously? You'd let me tag along?"

"Sure. Unless you'd rather spend the afternoon settling into your hotel room."

"Let's see." She tapped her unpainted lip with a fingertip as if seriously pondering the question. "I could spend the day raiding the minibar and watching talk shows about women who sleep with their husband's best friend and end up pregnant, only to discover the results of their pregnancy test on national television. Or I could be flying over the ocean looking for whales with you...

"Uh, that's no choice. I'd love to come with you."

"Terrific. I'll let the pilot know that there'll be one more passenger." Once in a blue moon, Adam thought as he turned onto the twisting highway leading down the coast, despite the calendar date to the contrary, Christmas really did come early.

5

BECAUSE SHE KNEW Adam would want to get in the air as soon as possible, while the sky over the coast was still clear, Meghann assured him that she wouldn't mind putting off going to the hotel until after they'd landed back in Shelter Bay. There was also the salient point that she wanted to spend as much time as possible with him, and being in the air offered far more privacy than staying in town.

A town that was all decked out for the holidays. As they drove down Harborview, beneath the tinseled garlands, wreaths with huge red bows hung on lampposts, and the colorful shops with seasonal windsocks flying and windows painted with holiday scenes, Meghann felt an internal click.

Although the sun was still shining, fairy lights were blinking all over town, as if welcoming her home. Despite her years of a forced gypsy lifestyle, for some reason, whenever she thought of home, she'd think of Shelter Bay.

"It looks like a Christmas card," she murmured as Adam stopped at a crosswalk to let an elderly couple cross from Take the Cake Bakery to a car parked by the seawall. Although they were bundled up beyond immediate recognition, the fact that they were holding hands gave them away.

"Oh, it's the Douchetts," she said, pleased that they still seemed well and happy.

"In their eighties and still holding hands," Adam confirmed. "They're one of the reasons, along with my work, that I've stayed single. As far as I'm concerned, they set the gold standard for what a marriage should be. A standard their grandsons have definitely carried on."

He told her about Sax and Kara. And Cole and Kelli. And how the youngest Douchett brother, J.T., who was the closest to their age, had married the Irish actress and filmmaker Mary Joyce, which Meghann remembered reading about. If she'd been writing contemporary romance, she probably couldn't have resisted a fictional take on the Marine and the movie star.

"So, you've never married?" Adam's Wikipedia entry hadn't mentioned a wife, but everyone knew those things were sketchy at best. And all the other articles Google had kicked up concentrated on his career achievements.

"Nope. I came close a couple times, but things just didn't work out." He glanced over at her as he pulled into the parking lot of the harbor at the south end of the bay. "How about you?"

"I was married for a short time. It didn't work out either." She didn't add that her only excuse for having made such a major life mistake was that at the time she'd been homesick and lonely and being with someone who might not be the perfect mate had seemed better than being alone.

"I'm sorry."

She shrugged. "It was a few years ago. Now those days seem more like a story I wrote rather than real life. At least we didn't have any children."

The red-and-white Cessna floatplane was waiting at the dock. As they pulled into a nearby parking space, the pilot came out of the Sea Mist Restaurant next door to the yacht club.

"Hey," he greeted them. "I figured you guys could use a lunch, so I had a couple fried seafood samplers boxed up for you—cod, shrimp, calamari, and crab bits with spicy French fries. I hope that's okay, ma'am," he said, as if realizing she might not be up for an entire meal of fried food.

"That sounds perfect." Just the smell wafting from the brown paper bag nearly had her mouth watering. "I had a way overpriced package of sunflower seeds on the flight." And her layover in Denver hadn't been long enough to grab as much as a salad from one of the kiosks by the gate.

"Air travel isn't what it used to be," he agreed cheerfully. "Which is why I'm happy to have my own wings."

After spending so many hours on commercial flights today, Meghann envied him.

Five minutes later, they were flying over the sea. A sea that opened up with vast spaciousness that wasn't visible from the beach, or even from the top of the cliffs.

"It's like looking for a needle in a haystack," she said from her back seat. Adam was sitting shotgun upfront, high-powered binoculars pointed out the window. Below them were windswept gray swells, splotched with flecks of white and black. How on earth were they supposed to find one misplaced whale in water that seemed to stretch to infinity?

"Even more difficult since there's so much that could be a whale," he agreed when she mentioned that problem. "The plane beats the hell out of the boat, but even from the air lots of things, like sailboats and kayaks can look like dorsal fins. And a wave's shadow can look like a whale. Which is partly why Orcas are colored the way they are. From above the black blends in with the dark water and from below, their white bellies blend in with the whitecaps and clouds. It's the perfect camouflage."

"Which isn't helpful," she said. Her eyes were feeling the strain from moving back and forth as the plane flew over the water. "What's that?" she asked, suddenly seeing something that could have been a whale. Or not.

"Where?"

"Three o'clock." She pointed. "Just to the right of that sea stack." Which meant what she saw might merely be a shadow from the towering, jagged spike of tree-topped rock that had once been part of the continent.

"It's a possibility," Adam decided. "Let's take her down a bit," he instructed the pilot.

Sea spray spotted the windshield as the floatplane nearly skimmed the breaking crests of the waves. The change in viewpoint had the form she'd seen disappear from their vision for a moment, then Adam spotted it.

"Damn," he said. "Good try, Meggie. But it's a cormorant."

Unfortunately, he was right. Perched on a log, the bird's tail had appeared to be a fin. As disappointed as she was to have been proven wrong about the whale/bird, Meghann felt a flush of pleasure at his seemingly unconscious use of her old nickname. Which only he had ever called her.

The first time had been after their Heathcliff argument. They'd been sitting cross-legged, face-to-face on his bed, and for one suspended moment, she'd seen something dangerous, like heat lightning on the horizon before a sea storm, flash in his gray eyes.

She'd drawn in a sharp breath and waited…

He'd bent his head toward her. As if connected by an invisible cord, she'd leaned toward him.

Her vision had blurred and her lips had part-ed instinctively, as they were now only a breath away. But then the grinding sound of the garage door opening as his mother had returned from the Cut Loose Salon, broke the suspended spell.

Unnerved, shaken, and needy in a way she'd never before felt, Meghann had dragged her hand through her hair and had returned to trying, unsucessfully it turned out, to explain the concept of the tortured, ill-behaved Byronic hero who'd been a literary fixture during the Romantic era.

"If that's truly the case, people back then had a really screwed up idea about romance," Adam had stated firmly. "I've always thought love should make someone feel better, Meggie. Not worse."

Having had no strong argument for that, and unsettled by the way he'd used a nickname no one else ever had called her before, which added yet more intimacy to their tutor-student relation-ship, Meghann had picked up the composition book and suggested he write down what he'd said, as if it had been an essay question on an SAT or his Cal-Poly early admission-application.

And yes, she'd assured him, even as he'd grumbled, punctuation counted.

And when he was finished, although she wasn't entirely prepared to give in, she hadn't been able to deny that he had a point. Because he'd always managed to make her feel better. Which was why, somehow, when she hadn't been paying attention, she'd fallen in love with him.

They stayed out over the water for an hour, during which time their quest seemed to feel more and more quixotic. The wind had picked up, blowing in from the north, bringing with it storm clouds pregnant with rain. Just ahead of them, the sun was lowering in the sky, sending blinding gold light into the windshield and glinting off the whitecaps in a way that cast more deceptive shadows.

"Let's go along the coast one last time," Adam instructed the pilot. "One report had him off Castaway Cove."

"If he swims into there, he'll be in trouble," Meghann said. "It's so shallow."

"Yeah. Then we could be looking at a beaching situation. But if he's out there, we'll find him."

Her mood, which had been sinking as fast as the winter sun, lifted a bit at his confidence. She also liked the fact that he'd included her in the search party. It made them seem like a team.

She had to fight back the laugh as a book title flashed through her mind: *Nerds in Love*.

Not that she was still in love with Adam Wayne. After all these years apart, that would be ridiculously illogical.

And while she might have been a book nerd who'd struggled to memorize the periodic table and he'd been a science geek who treated punctuation rules like mere suggestion, the one thing they'd definitely had in common was they were both nothing if not logical.

So why, she asked herself as the plane drifted over the Shelter Bay drawbridge, headed toward the dock, did she suddenly feel like that love-struck teenage girl she'd once been?

6

"I FEEL BAD we didn't find your missing whale," Meghann said as they drove from the harbor up the hill to the Whale Song Inn.

"I don't even know if there *is* a whale. Pacific Northwest Orcas are either coastal fish eaters, marine ocean mammal eaters, or offshores, whose diets and behaviors are a mystery," he told her. "The pod groups remain as separate as the houses in *Harry Potter* or lunch tables in a high school cafeteria. While Southern Orcas usually winter up in Puget Sound, in recent years smaller sub-clans have been spotted as far south as Monterey."

"So, what you're saying is that if a whale did get separated during migration, he could be anywhere?"

"That's about it."

"How long will you keep looking?"

"Good question." And one he hadn't figured

out for himself. "Orcas can swim a hundred nautical miles in a day. So, if a family group did for some reason decide to bypass their usual feeding grounds in Puget Sound, it wouldn't take them long to get down here. Once they go too much farther south, if he or she doesn't connect with them soon, then we're pretty much out of luck."

"It sounds as if he'd be, too."

"Yeah."

"Which is why, even if you do find him, you still need to find his pod."

"Which is also easier said than done. Some have been tagged with satellite trackers, but since Orcas like to brush up against rocks and even temporarily beach themselves to keep their bodies smooth for easier swimming, those trackers tend to get brushed off."

"Are you going out again on your boat to-night?"

"Yeah. But not for whale watching."

He pulled up in front of the turreted, ginger-bread-encrusted Victorian that harkened back to the days when Shelter Bay had catered to the rich and famous who'd traveled from as far away as Chicago and New York for the supposedly healing waters outside of town.

They'd had a short argument on the drive from Portland about her paying for the hotel room. Which he'd won when he'd assured her that since it was low season on the Oregon coast, the owners of the Whale Song, who just happened to be parents of three elementary school children, had comped the suite in return for her much-appreciated contribution to the science museum fund.

"My boat, the *Sea Wolf*, is in the holiday parade. It's good public relations to get people more involved in supporting efforts to create a world where every whale and dolphin—and killer whales are, actually, the largest of the dolphins—is safe and free."

"That's quite an admirable goal."

"One that's going to take a united international effort. The guy who set up the institute funding my work currently has marine biologists working in thirty-one different countries. I'm just a small cog in the machine."

"So you say. But I think it's wonderful. And I already see a story possibility."

"That would be great if you wrote something about it. You're reaching more people than I ever could. Some days my work seems to be as much about preaching the message as it does research."

"Thus tonight's parade."

"Yeah. The mayor got the idea last year, hoping it'd draw in tourists. I'm not sure it was all that successful bringing in any new money, but locals really enjoyed it, so it looks as if it's now going to be an annual Shelter Bay tradition."

"I always wanted to go to the one in Portland," she said. A little wistfully, Adam thought. He'd attended several times with his family over the years. If she'd only said something back then, he could have taken her. And, he heard Sax and Dillon's voices in his mind, maybe even gotten lucky.

"We don't have nearly the number of boats as Portland. But you're welcome to come with me."

"On your boat? Really?"

"Sure. Though I have to warn you, it's really cold out there at night."

"I told you, I can handle cold. I love the idea."

She wasn't the only one. Still…

"Your body's three hours ahead of Oregon," he reminded her.

"True. What time's the parade?"

"Six. But you know how time is relative in Shelter Bay."

"That's still only nine New York time," she pointed out. "And thanks to that ginormous fish sampler, I won't need dinner, so I'll be fine."

"You sure? That'll make for a really long day."

Damn. Why the hell did he keep warning her off? *Hashtag Shut Up.*

"I'm positive. Besides, I still have time for a nap."

This time the unbidden image flashing on that high-def screen in Adam's mind was of Meghann Quinn all warm and sleep-tousled in one of the inn's antique beds. Working at not imagining tangling the sheets with her as he held the glass door open, he fell back on the old trick of focusing his brain on reciting prime numbers.

"I used to work here," she murmured as they crossed the whitewashed pine floor.

"I remember." She'd worked as a maid to earn money for college. Despite having earned a scholarship and participation in a work-study

program, she'd still worked her tail off squirrel-
ing away money, which had always made him
feel a little guilty for having had things so easy.

"But it was painted in dark Victorian colors
with heavy furniture back then. These soft blue
and sand hues make it so much more inviting,"
she said. Since he'd already gotten the room key
before leaving for Portland this morning, they
were able to go straight to the old-fashioned
cage elevator. "Funny. I used to imagine coming
back and staying here someday."

"I remember that being part of the plan once
you became a rich and famous writer."

"I know I sounded unbearably pretentious
and schoolgirl silly, but—"

"I never found it silly at all," he said as they
rode up to the honeymoon suite on the top
floor. "Most people have dreams. But you
focused like a laser on making your dream a
goal. And here you are, just where you once
dreamed."

On cue, the elevator opened directly into the
suite painted in soft sea glass blues and greens.
The timing was so perfect Meghann wouldn't
have been surprised by a flare of trumpets
announcing her arrival.

She laughed softly as she walked over to a pair of French doors leading out onto a balcony that offered a dazzling view of the bay, sea, and the red-and-white striped Shelter Bay lighthouse.

"It's different," she said. "Not just the room but it feels so different being here as a guest, rather than dragging along a vacuum and a towering stack of fresh sheets and towels."

"It's all a matter of perspective. My family used to go sailing all the time." Adam crossed the room to stand beside her. "I pretty much grew up on the water."

He'd wanted to take her sailing that summer. He'd spent way too much time daydreaming about how she'd look in short shorts that would show off her legs, and a crop top, with her sunset-bright hair blowing free in the wind. He'd imagined how she'd taste with salt on her lips. And then, because he was a guy, he'd imagined casting anchor in some hidden cove and tasting a whole lot more.

But that would have been too much like a real date and he hadn't had the balls to ask. Because if she'd turned him down, their friendship could've been at risk.

There was also the case that his parents had

been very clear that the girl they'd hired to boost his English grade, a girl who didn't even have a family to call her own, wasn't anywhere near their social status. Small town strata, he'd discovered, was even more separated than the seas' Paleozoic and Mesozoic Eras.

He wondered what they thought about Meghann now. Not that he cared. Hell, he hadn't cared back then. At least for himself. But he'd known how frosty his mother could be and hadn't wanted to risk Meghann getting hurt. Jill, with her warm and open heart, had immediately taken to Meghann. His sister had been the one to tell him about her first book, which had hit the *New York Times* list right out of the gate.

"Being out on the water for whales is a lot different from sailing," he said, shaking off thoughts of opportunities missed. That was then. This was now. And if he had anything to say about it, this time things would be different.

She glanced up at him. "Is it less fun because it's work?"

"More fun. Because I don't take it for granted."

"That's nice. That we both ended up doing things that make us happy."

"Yeah. It is." The coconut scent of her shampoo reminded him of a tropical island. Which, in turn, had Adam imagining her wearing a grass skirt and doing the hula. Which just went to show that she wasn't the only one with an active imagination.

His jeans were growing too tight. Just like high school. "I'd better be going."

"I suppose so." She didn't sound any more eager to have him leave than he was to go.

"Okay." He rocked back on his heels. "How about I come back in an hour?"

"That'll work."

"Unless you'd rather just watch the parade from here." What are you doing? a voice shouted in his head. Shut. The. Fuck. Up.

She looked up at him. "No. I'd rather be in the parade than watch it. If you're absolutely certain it's okay with you."

"I wouldn't have asked if I hadn't meant it." Adam blew out a breath before turning around and heading back toward the door. "I'll take your suitcase into the bedroom."

"I can manage. Really. You should go finish getting your boat ready."

He glanced down at his watch, thinking of

those last strings of lights that were still sitting on the deck waiting to be strung. "Okay. How about I pick you up at five thirty?"

"I'll be ready."

Having undoubtedly impressed her with how his conversational skills had improved since the last time they'd been together, he escaped before the last of what remained of his brain turned completely to mush.

"Well," Meghann murmured after she shut the door behind him. "That could have gone better."

They'd gotten along so well out on the plane when he'd been telling her all about his work. But then he'd seemed to have distanced himself. Maybe he'd only invited her along on the plane because he hadn't wanted to waste the time of driving her to the inn? Perhaps she'd misinterpreted that look he'd given her in the airport, the one that a man gives a woman he's sexually interested in?

But if that were the case, why had he turned around and invited her out onto the boat tonight? Maybe because he'd felt sorry for her being stuck here in the suite alone while everyone else in town was out enjoying themselves?

"There's a reason you write YA," she muttered as she rolled her suitcase into the bedroom, where the lacey white iron bed seemed to dominate the room even more than it had back when she'd been changing the sheets. "Your social skills when it comes to men, at least Adam Wayne, haven't evolved past twelfth grade."

Which was a dismal thought. But unfortunately true.

Dammit, she hadn't flown all the way across the country just to hand out some books to raise money for a good cause. She'd come because, just like that Trisha Yearwood song, she'd lost Adam once. And dreamed about him. So many times over the intervening years.

She didn't want to leave Shelter Bay without at least exploring the possibility that this time things could end up differently.

She'd just finished unpacking and had turned down the duvet when there was a knock on the door.

Expecting the maid, checking to see if she needed any more towels or pillows, Meghann was surprised to see Adam standing in the doorway, as if conjured up by her unruly mind.

"I forgot something."

"Oh?" Maybe like asking her to the Snow Ball? "What?"

"This."

Without waiting for an invitation, he came back into the suite, kicked the door shut behind him and slid his fingers in her hair.

His eyes darkened to the turbulent hue of a stormy sea, reaching back across their years apart to a time when she'd spent a summer drowning in those hooded gray depths. The difference was that back then, his gaze had been unfathomable. As mysterious as the sea they'd flown over this afternoon.

Now, as he looked down at her, his expression more serious than she'd ever seen it, more serious than early in her tutoring when he'd suddenly realized that he might actually flunk English, which would keep him from graduation, more serious than it had been that last day they'd said goodbye for what seemed like the last time, and even more serious than earlier today when they'd been out looking for a possibly lost whale.

And thank you, God, as she read his intention written all over that handsome face in bold masculine script, she knew that just as they'd so often been, they were once again on exactly the same wavelength.

Meghann unconsciously parted her lips. Then drew in a breath, waiting as he cupped her face in his hands and lowered his head.

7

S HE COULDN'T HELP it. Just like one of the love-struck teens in her novels, her eyelids fluttered shut. Adam had told her that Orcas could hold their breaths while diving as long as twelve minutes. She was certain she was approaching that as he seemed determined to take his time.

And not in that hesitant, shy, geeky way he'd first kissed her beneath a night sky brilliant with summer constellations, but as a grown man very much aware of what he was doing.

"Do you know how long I've been waiting for this?"

She shuddered as he nipped an earlobe. "Since we landed at the dock?"

"Longer." His lips skimmed along her jaw, up her cheek, to her temple while his fingers splayed low on her back, drawing her closer.

"Since the airport?"

"Longer." His mouth finally moved back down to hers to suck at her lower lip as she wondered if it was, indeed, possible for a human being to melt.

Adam would know. He was, after all, a brainiac. A biologist. True, he studied marine mammals, but...

The only problem was that she couldn't have asked him if she'd wanted to, because as he tugged her even closer against him, her brain fogged and words deserted her. They fit together perfectly, all her soft parts molding against his hard chest, thighs, and, wow, parts of her that had gone neglected far too long against the stony erection below his belt.

"From that first day," he said in a deep, husky voice that vibrated through every cell in her body. "When you walked into homeroom." He nipped at her chin and made her whimper with need. "It was like looking at the aurora borealis."

"You never told me." No man had ever compared her to those shimmering Northern Lights that occasionally appeared on a rare clear night on the Oregon Coast.

"I know. I should have. But you terrified

me."

The stunning idea that wallflower her could have terrified any boy was such a revelation, Meghann couldn't have responded if she'd wanted to because finally (!!) his mouth claimed hers and he was kissing her long and hard, and she was holding tight to him, as if he were the only thing that could keep her from drowning.

And then, just as her mind was screaming at him to touch her, all over, and to take her now, he lifted his head, and as if not yet prepared to entirely let go, he put his hands on her waist as he took a step back.

"You need a nap."

"I need you." Relief that she hadn't entirely lost the power of speech tangled with the throbbing ache of body parts that, if they could've acted on their own, would've thrown themselves at Adam, taken him down, and had their way with him. Right here and now, on the thick ivory carpet.

"It's too soon."

"You said you've wanted me since that first day," she reminded him. She wasn't certain if she sounded needy or slutty. Neither did she care.

"I did." He kissed her again, and although it

wasn't as long, or as deep, it rocked her to the core. "I still do."

"We've an hour until the boat parade," she said silkily, channeling an inner seductress she hadn't even realized had been lurking inside her as she splayed her hand on the front of his Shelter Bay Whale Research sweatshirt.

His laugh was rough, ragged, and, damn it, regretful.

Then he saved her from feeling like a total failure.

"Forty-five minutes," he pointed out. "Which isn't nearly time for all the things I want to do to you. With you." He ran his hand down her side, from her breasts to her hips. "But after twelve long years of regretting letting you get away without seeing how we could have been together, I damn well want to do this right."

"Wow." She blew out a ragged breath. "Your prose skills have improved."

"I had a good tutor." His left hand moved to her back and pulled her close again. Conversation, especially about their relationship or sex, or worse yet, both in one sentence, would always cause her ex to deflate. Unsurprisingly, Adam was made of harder stuff—and no, that wasn't entirely a metaphor—than her former husband. "And a sexy muse."

Having had to "sell" herself to so many different foster parents over the years, Meghann knew both her strengths and her flaws. Being sexy was definitely not one of her attributes. But the fact that Adam believed her to be had her almost believing it herself.

"I've got to leave," he said, his tone letting her know it wasn't his first choice.

"I know." It wasn't hers either. "They say patience is a virtue."

"I've never known who *they* are." He trailed his knuckles up her cheek. "But whoever they are, they obviously have no idea how I'm feeling right now."

She could have him, Meghann realized. Right now. All it would take was a single word, a touch, and he'd bail on the boat parade in order to make love with her. She'd never, not once in her life, played the role of a seductress because, quite honestly, she'd never felt like one.

Her former husband had picked up on that insecurity the first day she'd shown up for his class. He'd used her need to be loved to control her in so many ways that it had taken her two years of marriage to realize that his manipulation wasn't born out of his superior strength, as she'd mistakenly believed, but his innate weakness. He could only feel strong by making others feel less so.

Adam, who'd never been one for nuances, had told her straight out how he felt. He'd never been adept at playing social relationship games. Nor had she. Which had been another thing that had bonded them back when social success had been the coin of the high school realm.

A book nerd, a brainiac science guy, and a misplaced killer whale. She laughed as a tag line for their story flashed into her mind.

"You realize," he said dryly, "laughing at a male in my situation can cause emotional and possibly even painful physical damage."

"Poor Adam." She went up on her toes and pressed her lips against his. "What if I promised to make it up to you later? After the parade?"

He pulled her closer again and gave her a slow, dreamy kiss that had her body humming.

"Take a nap," he said as he pulled back way too soon. He ran his hand down her hair. "Because you're going to need all your energy later."

And with that promise, he let himself out of the suite.

As she listened to the elevator cranking its way back down to the lobby, Meghann wondered how on earth he expected her to sleep after that exit line.

8

ALTHOUGH SHE WASN'T anywhere near the star level of Angelina Jolie or Taylor Swift, Meghann had been prepared for some public appearances. She and Adam had discussed possibilities during their drive down from Portland and one of the events during this holiday week she was looking forward to doing was speaking to students, not just about how to become a writer but about the importance of following their dreams.

Adam had spent time on the phone with Ginger Wells, principal of Shelter Bay High School. And with Mrs. Lessman, who'd been teaching AP English back when Meghann was in school. After that, he'd made a couple more calls to CCC. Before they'd gotten to Newberg an hour later, they'd arranged for her to appear to students from both schools the day after Christmas at the restored historical Art Deco

Orcas Theater. Which was, Adam informed her, where Irish movie star Mary Joyce had once spoken.

Not sure she could live up to that billing, Meghann was looking forward to the Q-and-A part of the presentation, when she'd get to speak one-on-one with attendees. Adam had assured her that she'd fill every seat in the place, which she'd thought was overly optimistic.

Until she arrived at the dock for the parade and was bombarded by both adults and teens thrusting out books for her to sign.

Finally, when it looked as if she'd be single-handedly responsible for holding up the parade, she was happy to let Adam step in to tell every-one that she was needed on the boat and they'd have plenty of opportunities to talk with her and have her sign copies on the twenty-sixth at the Orcas Theater.

"Thank you," she said as he helped her onto the white thirty-eight-foot *Sea Wolf.* "This is really nice." She was surprised by how sleek and modern the boat had been fitted out. Although all the gauges and dials and other equipment pointed to it being a research vessel rather than a pleasure boat, the only thing she could see that differentiated it was the bunks rather than beds in the two sleeping staterooms.

"It's a lot better than many research vessels," he said. "And more compact. It's part of the small boat fleet so we can get in and out of all the coves along the coast. It's also been sound-proofed so it can run silent, like Navy submarines."

"So you don't disturb the whales." Having spent four years living in Shelter Bay, she'd learned how noise from boats not only stressed whales out but could seriously interfere with their ability to communicate.

"Got it in one. There aren't that many boats as well tricked out as this one, but the guy who funds the institute has deep pockets."

After undocking, he idled out to where the other vessels, from sea kayaks to a fishing boat were lining up, waiting for the habormaster's signal. As three sharp blasts of an air horn came across the water, all of them turned on their lights.

"Oh!" Meghann felt six years old as the night lit up with a dazzling display of colored lights as varied as the boats and the owners themselves. "It's wonderful!"

There were the typical Christmas displays: lighted trees, snowmen, angels, Santa's sleigh, and a manger. A huge goose, outlined in blue, wearing a red scarf, appeared to fly off the stern of a sailboat. The fishing boat had a giant red Dungeness crab opening and closing its claws.

Which was admittedly impressive and fun. But when it came to the best, the *Sea Wolf* would get her vote. "You must have spent hours on it," she said.

He shrugged. "I designed it last year and since it proved popular and migration is my busiest time, I decided just to repeat it. The mechanics to make the whales move are new this year. I added them the day before yesterday and finished putting on the outline lights this afternoon."

The boat was outlined, bow to stern, in white lights while a mother and baby whale, lit in blue, appeared to breach from the bow.

"I love it."

"Thanks. We came in second last year, behind the Douchetts' crab. They won with those moving claws, which is partly why I decided to add animation."

"Not that you're competitive or anything."

"Who? Me?"

They shared a laugh, then, as they chugged around the harbor, Meghann enjoyed the applause and oohs and aahs of the crowd who'd packed onto bleachers and watched from the brightly lit patio of the Sea Mist Restaurant and the upper deck of the yacht club. Others, not fortunate enough to have nailed seats, seemed equally happy to line the dock.

"It's as if all of Shelter Bay has shown up," she said.

"Small towns," he said. "Not much else to do on a winter night."

"That's not it." As much as she loved the fancifully decorated store windows and Rockefeller Plaza during the holidays, Shelter Bay's boat parade touched some hidden core deep inside her. "This is special. I can't believe Portland's parade could be any better."

His laugh was deep and rich. "We have twenty-five boats. They average around sixty each year. With many professionally decorated."

"Which shouldn't count," she said. "This is special because people cared enough to do the work themselves for others to enjoy. Not show off."

"I doubt that everyone in the city just wants to show off," he said. "But yeah. This feels special. Like home."

That was it, Meghann realized. She'd experienced that comfortable familiarity as they'd driven down Harborview earlier today. She'd enjoyed seeing the town, looking like a toy train layout from the air. But now, as she waved a mittened hand back at the crowd, who was waving at them, for the very first time in her life, Meghann Quinn felt as if she'd come home.

*   *   *

THEY'D JUST DOCKED when they were approached by a sixty-something woman wearing a thick quilted red parka and a dark-haired man with a faint limp who was holding hands with a woman wearing a red coat and knit cap atop glossy black curls. Accompanying them were a blonde little girl dressed from head to toe in pink, adolescent boys who appeared to be identical twins, and an elderly man.

Adam greeted them, and after introductions had been made, the older woman, Dee Kentta, said, "I brought Mac and Annie and the kids to tell you the captain showed up at their house right before they left for the parade."

The house in question, Adam knew, was the Culhane's yellow Victorian on Castaway Cove.

"I saw him," Emma, the little girl, piped up. "He was rubbing on the rocks. I was afraid he'd hurt himself, so I went and got my big brothers."

Adam turned toward the boys, Justin and Jordan. Jordan, the oldest by two minutes, had taken a class he'd taught this past summer at the Newport Aquarium about the evolution that had taken whales from land mammals to the sea fifty million years ago. "Was it dark yet? And you're sure it was an Orca and not a dolphin?" At deep dusk, there could be a resemblance.

"The sun hadn't set yet," Jordan said. "And yessir, it was definitely an Orca."

"I saw it, too," Annie Culhane said. "I was in the bedroom getting ready to leave when the boys called. I looked out the window and there he was."

"It's the captain," Dee insisted. "Just like I told you."

"Did you see any other whales in the vicinity?" he asked Jordan and Annie.

"No," they said together.

"He was all alone," Emma agreed. "Poor thing. Jordan told me all about whales. He says they travel in families called pods."

"That's true."

"So are you going to help him find his family? He must be lonely. And it's even worse to be all alone at Christmas."

Everyone was looking at him. Even Meggie. Waiting for his answer. Waiting, Adam knew, for him to do something. After all, he was the only whale expert here at the moment.

"I'm going to do my best," he said. "But the sky's too cloudy tonight for the floatplane. And the fog's rolling in, so it'd be hard to see anything from the boat."

"But he's all alone." Emma Culhane's voice was close to a whine. "And Orcas always stay with their mommies. Even when they're all grown up. So his mommy must be *terribly, horribly* worried about him."

"He'll be all right," her father, Mac Culhane, midnight deejay for KBAY radio assured his daughter.

"He won't be the first Orca to come along up close to the coast," Charlie, Mac's grandfather, said. "I've seen more than a few in my day, rubbing against the rocks. And they probably come here for the same reason folks do. It's a nice place to visit."

"Yeah," the other boy, Justin, said. "Maybe he wants to buy one of those *I went whale watching in Shelter Bay* T-shirts."

Emma fisted her small hands at the waist of her pink coat and tossed up her chin. "Whales can't wear T-shirts, silly."

"You going out tomorrow at first light?" Dee pressed.

Adam glanced over at Meghann, whose expression was not only resigned but told him that she was on Dee's side. However they spent tonight, they were not going to be having a leisurely breakfast in bed afterwards.

"It's Christmas Eve," he pointed out.

"Like whales keep social calendars," Dee scoffed.

"If it is the captain, maybe he just wants to hang around through the holidays, then he'll be on his way," Adam said. From Dee's scowl and the way her dark brows dove toward her nose, he knew he hadn't exactly hit a home run with that suggestion.

"I'll go out," he said. "But not until the fog

lifts."

"And we'll call if we see him again," Mac Culhane said.

"Can I come with you?" Jordan asked.

"Me, too?" Justin, whom Adam knew to be more interested in music and playing with his garage band, asked.

"Sure," Adam agreed. At this point he wasn't even sure what he'd do if he found a misplaced whale, but locating him would be the first step.

"I want to go, too!" Emma began bouncing up and down as if those Barbie-pink boots had springs in the rubber soles.

"I need you at home to help wrap presents," her mother said, obviously attempting to distract her. "I thought you could color some designer paper."

"You already brought paper home from your scrapbook store. I want to see the whale again. I like whales because they sing." She turned to Meghann. "Daddy bought me a CD of their songs. I play it *all* the time. Don't I, Mommy?"

"You certainly do," Annie said with a wry smile that suggested the child wasn't exaggerating about the frequency.

"I'd like to hear it someday," Meghann said.

"You can come over to our house."

"That sounds like fun. Meanwhile, I need to do some last-minute shopping tomorrow. I thought I might stop and have a cupcake, but it'd be nice to have some help choosing which flavor."

"I could do that! Couldn't I, Mommy?"

"You certainly could." Annie smiled at Meghann, silently thanking her for sidetracking her daughter.

"My new favorite is the chocolate candy cane," Emma said. "It's scrumptious!"

"It definitely sounds Christmassy," Meghann agreed.

"I'm sure you've got a packed schedule, since you're here as a celebrity, but if you have time for lunch, Emma and I would love to have you join us at Chef Maddy's Lavender Hill Farm Restaurant."

"Actually, I mostly came here to visit old friends." The look she slanted Adam's way told everyone exactly which old friend in particular she was referring to. "The only official events planned are a public talk the day after Christmas at the theater and an appearance to hopefully boost participation in the auction at the Snow

Ball." Which, Adam realized as she shot him a quick, questioning glance, he still hadn't asked her to. "So, I'd love to have lunch with you."

"Free at last," Adam said as they escaped the group and walked, hand in hand to the SUV.

"I liked them," Meghann said.

"So do I. But I thought they'd never leave. And with me now having to leave at the crack of dawn to avoid Dee hounding me for the rest of my days if I don't find her whale, I don't want to waste any time getting you back to your hotel so I can finally seduce you."

"Ha!" She shook her head and flashed a sassy, sexy grin. "What if I want to seduce you?"

He grinned back and ducked his head, giving her a quick kiss that drew hoots of approval from spectators leaving the parade. "Works for me."

9

ADAM KNEW THAT despite time-travel fiction stating the contrary, most people thought of time as a universal constant. Einstein had proven that time was, indeed relative. But nothing in Einstein's Theory of Relativity could adequately explain why the drive to the Whale Song Inn from the harbor took forever.

As did the walk across the lobby, which also defied both the rules of architecture and Shelter Bay's zoning laws by having lengthened to a mile long since they'd left for the boat parade.

As soon as the brass elevator gate closed, Adam leaned down and kissed her. Her lips were smooth as silk and chilled from being outdoors. But as she leaned in and kissed him back, they began to warm. And soften.

"People can see us," she murmured as he nipped at her bottom lip.

"Ask me if I care." His hands settled on her

waist as he kissed her again, keeping it light for propriety's sake. Not that he cared what people might say. Having spent most of his younger years as being seen as "different" by the time he'd reached high school he'd quit trying to fit in. Until he'd met Meggie. Who was just different enough herself to accept him for who he was.

At least she'd let him kiss her. He'd spent a lot of time looking at the unnaturally endowed women in comic books—and the rare *Playboy* or *Penthouse* one of the guys in science club would snag from his dad's stash—and had imagined what touching a woman, kissing her, having sex with her would feel like.

He and Meggie hadn't made it to that last part, but he had discovered, the first time her lips had softened beneath his, that his imagination regarding kissing hadn't even come close to reality. Proving the old adage about reality never matching up to the fantasy dead wrong.

She'd surpassed it. So much so, that, although he'd been with other women over the intervening years—he might be a nerd, but he wasn't a monk—none of them had ever made him feel as if he were in danger of spontaneous combustion the way Meghann Quinn had.

And still did. Since they seemed to be breaking all sorts of natural laws, Adam wouldn't have been at all surprised to look up and see an entire Milky Way of constellations swirling overhead.

Unlike Adam's earlier hot, demanding kiss, this one was so meltingly sweet. Tender and filled with promise. As Meghann swayed toward him to kiss him back, memories wrapped them in glistening silken ribbons and she wouldn't have been at all surprised to hear the twitter of little blue cartoon bluebirds circling overhead.

When he deepened the kiss, his beard scraping her cheek, his tongue sweeping her mouth, all Meghann could think was that although she'd never considered herself hot, at the moment that was precisely the right word because between the time they'd entered the elevator and now, as the door opened into her suite, the blood flowing in her veins had turned to flames.

Adam Wayne had been valedictorian of his graduating class, which hadn't surprised anyone. During the summer of their *The Notebook* romance (if Noah had been written as a rich boy and Allie had been an impoverished foster kid, without World War Two and dementia darkening the teen love story), his kisses had been so sweet. Almost grateful.

But wow, he must have had a lot of practice during their time apart, because if that Swedish Nobel Prize committee gave away awards for kissing, he would have won it, hands down.

And speaking of hands, after they'd thrown their coats onto the sofa immediately upon entering the suite, he cupped her butt, and with his shoulder and arm muscles bunching, he lifted her up against him just like Noah had Allie in that hot and heavy kissing in the rain scene from *The Notebook*. A reunion that hadn't turned out nearly as well as Adam's and hers. So far.

She wrapped her legs—which probably were no longer capable of holding her upright—around his waist, and kissed him back as he carried her into the bedroom where he put her on the bed.

Then, hitting the pause button, he stood there, looking down at her, his gaze as serious as she'd ever seen it. Even more so than that night they'd built a fire on the beach and as sparks from the logs had flown upward into a star-spangled sky, had talked until dawn about all the things working against a long-distance relationship. And how, rather than end up eventually hurting each other, the sensible, *logical* thing to do was to accept the summer for what it had been and be grateful for the memories.

The only problem was that she hadn't felt at all logical then. And didn't now.

"I made a mistake," he said.

"This isn't a mistake." There was no way she was going to let him get away with any analytical argument this time!

His lips quirked at one corner. His gray eyes warmed with a sexy mixture of lust and humor. "Not tonight. Back then."

"You're not going to get any argument from me."

"One of the things I've learned is that sometimes logic sucks."

"I'm not going to argue that, either." She met his gaze. "But I will let you make it up to me."

"I intend to." The mattress sighed as he sat down beside her and ran his hand down her leg. "But first I want to get one thing straight."

His fingers were making little figure eights, which he'd undoubtedly think of as infinity loops, at the inside of her thigh. Even as she wanted to scream at him to please stop talking and just get on with the program, Meghann swallowed hard and said, "Okay."

"This isn't a vacation fling. And it isn't just living out an unfulfilled teen romance. It's real. And whatever happens, unless you decide I'm the worst lover you've ever had and never want to be with me again, this isn't the end. But a beginning."

"What if I turn out to be the worst lover *you've* ever had?"

"Not." He punctuated the word with a light kiss. "Going." Another kiss. "To." And another. "Happen." One more.

That said, he unzipped her jeans and pulled them down her legs, while she yanked her sweatshirt over her head. Her underwear was next, then she was on her knees, lifting up his shirt, exposing a ripped, dark torso that, were it featured on the cover of one of her books would have had copies flying off shelves. Who knew that whale research could be so physical?

He stood up and dragged his jeans down his legs, followed by a pair of red (!!) boxer briefs that definitely hinted at hot, hidden depths.

Desperate to get him on her, *in* her, she

grabbed his hands and pulled him back down onto the bed.

"I want to take this slow," he reminded her again. "Make it last."

Easy for him to say.

But apparently determined to set the pace, Adam linked their hands together then raised them to the white iron headboard and curled her fingers around the lacy filigree.

Time slowed as his clever hands touched her everywhere. As his mouth followed the trail those hands had blazed. He caressed. Ravished. Loved.

And then, after he'd brought her to a high peak, and sent her tumbling into a dazzling explosion of light and heat, he took her up again. And again.

Finally, just when she didn't think she could take any more, Adam allowed her to turn the tables, teasing, tasting, tormenting, moving around the bed, staying just out of reach, until it was his turn to beg for release.

Which Meghann gave him. Eventually.

"I think you killed me," he said as they lay in a tangle of arms and quivering legs, waiting for their hearts to slow to a halfway-normal rhythm.

She trailed her fingers down his damp wash-board chest. Which had her wishing she'd let Caro drag her to the gym more often. Nature had blessed her with a long, lean body. Unfortunately, too many hours spent seated at a computer had admittedly left certain parts a bit...well, she couldn't deny it...jiggly.

"You said you wanted to take things slow."

"I did." He cupped her breasts, lifting them to his lips before pressing a line of kisses down her torso to her stomach, which she was too satiated to bother to suck in. Not that he seemed to notice. Or care.

Which was another surprise. After all these years of waiting, Meghann had secretly worried that they'd be a bit uncomfortable afterwards. But no, they were as easy and natural with each other as they'd ever been. As if no time at all had passed, they'd fallen right back into a friendship that had made the sex all the richer.

"Tell me about your marriage," he asked quietly.

Oh, and wasn't that perfect timing? Then again, now that they'd moved their relationship to a much more intimate level, she decided that he was entitled to know the story of how pitiful she'd been.

"It's pretty much a cliché. I was in college and a professor was very complimentary about my writing. He said I had a great future as a novelist."

"So at least he got that right."

"I suppose that depends. Even though I'd gone most of my life without a family, New York was like landing on a foreign planet. At least, in Oregon, I knew the landscape. So, I found myself totally at sea when he plucked me out of a comparative prose fiction class. Apparently he mentored one student each semester, and given the talent pool, I was hugely grateful to have been selected."

"Since I knew you'd make it back when we were in high school, I hate to suggest that you being young, gorgeous, and probably more naive than a lot of students had anything to do with it. But—"

"I know." She sighed. "You don't have to say it. I was star-struck, but it really was a wonderful opportunity. Even if I did have to unlearn much of what he taught me when I actually decided to write genre fiction. Which was the problem. He never accepted my work as 'real' novels."

"How many books has he published?"

"He's edited some anthologies of historical literary fiction."

"By historical, you mean that the writers were all dead, right?"

"Technically."

"Even writers aren't immortal, unless you believe in vampires and zombies," he said. "They're either dead or alive."

"All right. Yes. They were dead."

"So all he basically did was republish their work and get the credit."

"You realize you're making me feel really stupid."

"Not stupid. Never that. Maybe naive," he repeated. "And probably too trusting for your own good."

Call her perverse, but Meghann actually liked that they were still able to argue without taking away from their feelings for one another. Something she'd never been able to do with her husband, who always had to be right about everything.

"He was very well respected."

"He sounds like a jerk. And maybe a predator, hitting on his students. I have a hard time believing that's acceptable. Even in New York."

"Romantic relationships are discouraged because of the imbalance of power—"

"Gee, you think?"

"Do you want to hear this or not?"

"I'm sorry." He waved a hand. "Carry on. But I have to say that if I'd been there, I would've had to punch the guy's lights out."

"Ah, we're back to the *Die Hard* model of showing emotion."

Adam didn't argue that point. "Pushing him out a window would also be a good idea. After I kicked out his lung."

The idea of Adam beating up her ex-husband would have been humorous. If it weren't for his rock-hard eight pack (who knew there were two extra packs beyond six?) and if it didn't admittedly seem sexy. In a chauvinistic alpha-male sort of way. Like nerdy Peter Parker turning into superhero Spiderman.

"Getting back to the topic, romances weren't officially prohibited. And Anthony—"

"That was his name?"

"Anthony Leicester-Ravensdale.

"Get out. You're shitting me."

"No. That was really his name."

"Hell, Meggie, you didn't stand a chance. You moved all the way across the country to run into Mr. damn Darcy."

She'd gotten to the point that she could laugh. "I wish we'd stayed in touch," she said wistfully. "I could've used a laugh back then."

"You've no idea how much I wish that, too. Even if you would have been forced to bail me out of jail for assault and battery on a stick-up-the-butt snob."

"How did you know about the stick?"

"I'm a scientist. I spend my life dealing with deductive reasoning."

"Anthony was never physically abusive."

"Just emotionally," he suggested through gritted teeth. He was actually furious on her behalf. How amazingly wonderful was that?

"He belittled my work," she admitted. "Not just privately but every chance he got. It got so I dreaded going to faculty events because I knew he'd manage to get in at least one little dig about 'Meghann's little stories.'" Which was one of the nicer descriptions. Trite, derivative, rubbish, and a waste of trees were others that she decided, from the way Adam's left hand had curled into an unconscious fist, not to share.

"He's a douche. You're lucky to be rid of him."

"I know. But mostly because if I was still with him, I wouldn't be here with you." She cuddled closer, noticing the grit digging into her butt for the first time. "We got sand in the bed." She lifted a hand to her stiff hair. "And my hair is crunchy."

He grabbed a handful and put it into his mouth, testing. "Salty," he agreed. He untangled himself, stood up and held out a hand, bending down like a footman to a duchess. Escaping Jane Austen mentality was not easy, she thought with an inner sigh.

"There are extra sheets in the closet." He told her nothing she didn't remember from her days as a maid. "First, what would you say to a shower?"

She took his hand. "Given my choice between one of those billionaires who are such a romance staple these days and a hot guy with a brilliant mind, I'll take hot and brilliant anytime."

10

HAVING ALREADY EXCHANGED gifts with everyone she knew in New York, including buying fashionista Caro a racy red Alexander Wang Rocco bag, Meghann had realized during the boat parade that she didn't have anything for Adam. Nor did she have a clue what he would like. Or need. His choice in clothing didn't appear to have changed that much from high school, other than the fact that he no longer had a geeky Star Wars key ring hanging from his jeans.

"He's over for dinner a lot on nights Mac doesn't work at the station," Annie told her over a scrumptious warm squash, apple, and lentil salad. "Mac, whose motto is friends should never let friends listen to pop, has expanded his play list from classical and electronica to more country, but I'm not sure what CDs or downloads he has. I know he's a huge reader, so you can never go wrong with a book."

"Science fiction, I suppose." Another thing that apparently hadn't changed.

"Actually, now that I think about it, he and Mac were talking about a contemporary western mystery they'd both read."

"I saw a book sticking out of his backpack when he came for Thanksgiving dinner," Emma, who'd opted for the mac and cheese, said. "It had a boy and girl kissing on the cover."

"Really?"

"It was one of yours," Annie divulged. "*The Nerd Next Door.*" She grinned. "I read it myself and could totally see Adam in the boy."

Yikes. Had she been that transparent? And if so, had Adam recognized himself? Uh, like the stargazing lecture while the girl was waiting to be kissed wasn't a dead giveaway? Note to self: stop stealing from your real life.

"Everything's fair game to writers," she admitted. "But that was totally fiction."

"Of course it was," Annie agreed, even as it was obvious that she was dying to ask how much of the girl had been Meghann. "But to be honest, I suspect that while I love young adult fiction for the emotional depth—"

"Because everything is life and death at that age," Meghann interjected.

"Isn't that the truth?" She smiled toward Emma, who'd been temporarily distracted by a sea gull who'd dropped an oyster onto the patio outside the window and was proceeding to pick it apart. "This one's already so dramatic, I figure the coming years will be interesting."

"That's one way of putting it."

Annie's smile faded and a shadow came across her eyes. "I never thought I'd have children. And now I have three." The smile came blazing back like a summer sun, burning away the shadow. "So, whatever happens, it's all good."

"That's lovely."

Although she'd never met a man she'd want to have a child with and figured she had a few years yet before she had to worry about her eggs getting old, Meghann had been too focused on her writing to think about having children herself. But she had to admit that a little girl like Emma or a boy with shaggy bangs hanging down over serious gray eyes that observed the world from behind Harry Potter glasses would be nice. Better than nice, she considered. Someday...

"Anyway," Annie continued, "my point was that I suspect Adam only reads those books because you wrote them. The same way I started listening to KBAY more to hear the Mac at Midnight show than the country songs. That's pretty much how we communicated in the beginning. We'd talk a few minutes off the air between songs, then he'd send me messages by his song choice."

"Clever," Meghann said.

"I was coming off a divorce and gun shy." Annie shrugged. "And Mac was a divorced single dad trying to figure things out. I think it was safer for both of us. And we definitely talked more openly before we met in person than most people probably do their first few dates."

"Adam and I have a history."

"So I heard. You were his tutor."

"In English."

"And you loved him."

Meghann took a sip of the ruby merlot she'd ordered with lunch. "And you figured that out how?"

"It was obvious from the book. Which may

be fiction, but putting it together with the chemistry between the two of you I saw last night, and that kiss, well, I'd say that you've both kindled old flames."

"We didn't have any flames back then," Meghann admitted. "Just embers."

"Well, then." Annie lifted her glass. "Here's to second chances."

"Second chances," Meghan echoed.

*   *   *

HAVING BEEN TOLD that Adam liked western mysteries, Meghann dropped into Tidal Wave Books and bought a copy of C.J. Box's latest in his Joe Pickett series. There could be a problem if Adam hadn't bought her a gift, she belatedly realized. Which was not really a problem since being a longtime fan of Wyoming game warden Joe Pickett herself, she could always read it.

And who would have guessed that a girl who read Jane Austen and a boy who knew all the Star Trek books by number, would have a fictional genre in common? Making her wonder again how things might have turned out if they hadn't separated.

That was then. This was now. And for now,

she was looking forward to a romantic Christmas Eve when her phone buzzed. Speaking of her hottie nerd…

"They were right," Adam said without preamble after she'd swiped open her phone.

"You found him?"

"No. He slipped by us. Dee called to let me know he's in the harbor."

"You're kidding." She waved a hand he couldn't see. "Never mind." She thought of all the boats chugging in and out with so many people taking advantage of an unusually sunny Christmas Eve on the water. "Now what?"

"That's still to be determined. But meanwhile, I'm afraid our private holiday celebration is going to have to be postponed."

"No problem." She glanced over at Annie, who, from her expression, was apparently receiving the same message from the twins on *her* phone. "I'll meet you there."

She was waiting for Adam when the *Sea Wolf* arrived back at the dock. The word had, unsurprisingly, spread, and people had flocked to the harbor to watch the black-and-white Orca that was providing live entertainment.

"That's spyhopping," Emma said, pointing

as the whale bounced around, the top half of his body sticking vertically out of the water. "I saw it on the DVD Jordan brought home from his whale class. He's probably looking around for his family." Her excitement flagged at that idea. Like helium escaping a bright pink balloon. "Poor thing."

"It's good that he's here," Annie assured her daughter. "Now that Adam knows where he is, he'll be able to take care of him."

"And get him back with his mommy?"

Annie exchanged a look with Meghann. Although her tone had remained reassuring, her eyes were as concerned as Meghann herself was.

"Adam is the best," she hedged, obviously not wanting to make a promise she couldn't keep.

"It's the captain," Dee, who didn't seem the least bit surprised to see a whale hopping among all the pleasure boats, said. "I told Adam he was here to brighten his family's holiday."

"His family is out in the ocean," Emma said with a frown.

"That may be his whale family," Dee allowed. "But his human family is here and his spirit has come to be with them."

"Really?" The little girl's eyes widened. "Like a ghost?"

"Like a spirit," Dee corrected. "A friendly spirit."

"Like Caspar." Emma nodded. "I've seen the cartoons on TV. Though lots of people are afraid to be his friend because he looks spooky, there's no one nicer. Just like Orcas."

Dee tilted her head and looked down at the blonde sprite. "You're a smart little girl."

"I know," Emma agreed.

Meghann left them discussing spirit animals to meet Adam as he climbed off the boat. "Well, at least you won't have to be stuck out there in the fog and cold anymore," she told him, trying to find a bright spot in all this. "Because he's come to you."

"Which isn't much help since there's no way his pod is going to come in here," he said grimly. "And I don't even want to think about him getting sliced up by boat propellers."

"I hadn't thought of that." The idea was horrible and as bad as it would be for the whale, witnessing such a thing could undoubtedly leave emotional scars on all the children who were beginning to arrive at the dock. "Do you have a plan?"

"Not yet," he admitted. "The bottom line is to reunite him with his pod. There have been instances of driving a whale into a net, then lifting it up and moving it by truck. Or plane."

"That sounds terrible!"

"It's not ideal." Adam rubbed the back of his neck. "And definitely as last resort. Some facilities around the world are still borrowing or trading breeding whales and even when they're put into tanks and monitored, it's still life threatening. Which is why nearly fifty airlines, including some major, but unfortunately not all, U.S. carriers will no longer fly them."

"That definitely doesn't sound like very friendly skies." Meghann was appalled at the idea of this poor lost Orca being forced into a net and stuck on truck or plane. "So, how are you going to safely get him to go where you want him to?" she asked.

"It's problematic. Since you can't exactly call a wild whale over like you can a dog. One thing we've got going for us is that Orcas are incredibly social creatures."

"Is it a male or female?"

"It's too early to tell. Whales grow at pretty

much the same rate as humans. Once they hit adolescence, the male fins grow so fast that they're called sprouters. That's the main difference between sexes. Males have much larger dorsal and pectoral fins. For a long time marine biologists tried to figure out why an animal genetically designed to be so sleek, whose skin has been created to have laminar flow, which allows it to move through the water without a ripple, would grow such bulky, oversized fins that only slow it down. Guess what the general consensus turned out to be?"

"What?"

He winked. "That the girls like them."

Despite the seriousness of the situation, Meghann laughed.

11

FOR A TIME it would have been easy to forget that the whale was in a perilous situation. He swam around the bay, diving, and popping out of the water, spyhopping, squeaking and clicking in an obvious attempt to communicate.

Every so often he'd breach, flying out of the water with a gigantic rush, drenching everyone nearby, twisting to show off his white belly, then crashing back down again, disappearing beneath the water, only to pop up somewhere else and enjoying himself, seeming to laugh. Once he even dove down and returned with a fish, which he showed off before swallowing it.

It didn't take long until people were feeling moved to interact. When one woman, standing on the edge of the dock reached out her hand, causing the whale to come over and nuzzle her, others wanted to get into the act.

Which forced Adam, who'd told Meghann this had been one of his worries, to get on a loudspeaker to explain to everyone that although yes, it was obvious that the Orca was trying to socialize, the best thing they could do was not to get physically involved. So please, no touching. Not just for their own safety, but for the whale's well-being. Because he wasn't a pet to play with but a wild mammal who was going to be reunited with his family.

"Just like Willy," Emma, basking in her whale knowledge, explained to those around her.

The whale's behavior continued into the night. Most people, deciding nothing was going to happen anytime soon, left for home to get some sleep before Christmas morning. Others headed to midnight mass at St. Andrews, appropriately named for the patron saint of fishermen.

Adam, of course, stayed with the Orca. And even though she was still feeling a bit of jetlag, no one on the planet could have convinced Meghann to leave him.

*   *   *

ALTHOUGH YOU COULDN'T see it due to the heavy fog draping the harbor, according to

Adam's sea chart, the sun rose at seven fifty-three on Christmas morning. Seven minutes later, the bells at the town's four churches began to ring.

Shortly before dawn, what had been the Orca's conversational rising and falling riff of sounds began to turn more strident, more growing more and more urgent. Like an human newborn who couldn't be soothed no matter how many miles of pacing, lullabies sung, and hours of back-stroking.

By ten o'clock, as people began returning to the docks to check on their visitor, the cries were nearly nonstop.

"He's telling us he needs our help," Meghann said when Adam returned from talking with Dee and some of the tribal elders who'd also spent the night, eschewing Adam's offer of bunks in the boat to camp on the dock to be nearer the captain.

The cries were breaking her heart. Meghann could actually feel the pain. Only the most cold-hearted person wouldn't be moved by his desperation.

"I know. And we're trying," Adam said, an edge of frustration sharpening his voice. "Hell."

He yanked off his ball cap and dragged a hand through his bedhead. "I'm sorry."

"You don't have to apologize to me." Although she'd drifted off a few hours after midnight, he'd been up all night, talking on the radio with anyone he could find who might have a suggestion.

"We did have a stroke of luck. A volunteer watcher up in Washington was doing a count of our little guy's family unit and noticed that Moclips, one of the females, is missing a child. Since Orcas are the predators of the sea, and it's unlikely anything would attack a pod, we're assuming that it's him."

"How did he get separated?"

"There's no telling. But this is a really helpful thing because now we know his language."

"His language?"

"Whales are intensely social animals, probably even more social than those of us who study them."

"I wouldn't be so quick to judge," Meghann said. "You were certainly social enough the other night."

That earned a smile, as she'd hoped. "I'm sounding too pedantic again, aren't I?" he asked.

"Like the night of the star lecture."

"I enjoyed that night," she hedged. "At least the kiss… Tell me more about the plan."

"Well, like I said, they're super social, which is the reason for their huge brains that allow them to manage their various social groups, differentiate between other whales, and respond according to their situation. Also like people, they have their own languages. Northern whales can't speak to southern, and even within groups they have the equivalent of our regional accents.

"A volunteer watcher sent me a recording of this particular pod group. So, I'm hoping that if our guy hears his family, he'll want to leave to go to them."

"That sounds logical. But how do you make it happen?"

"I'm going to go out in the *Sea Wolf* and play the recordings beneath the water as I head out toward the ocean…

"Meanwhile, Cole Douchett's taking his fishing boat to where the satellite tracking says the pod should be. He's going to play hydrophone recordings we took yesterday and this morning of our whale. Since pods are multi-generational matrilineal, and Emma was right about even adult males following the females, hopefully the mom will head in toward shore to reclaim her child.

"Then they can all have a happily-ever-after reunion having themselves a fresh salmon Christmas dinner. While we get on with ours."

"You're not talking about dinner."

"No." He kissed her, a slow kiss with enough tongue to promise more. "I was thinking more about *our* reunion."

The idea, on top of that kiss, had her toes curling in her boots. "Do you think the plan will work?" She wished he'd looked more optimistic when he'd been describing it.

"I've no idea," he answered honestly. "Fortunately, killer whales are the loudest creatures in the sea, so they shouldn't have any trouble hearing each other's calls. So I'm damn well going to try."

As word circulated throughout the area, more and more people arrived. Kara Douchett, who had her deputies out directing traffic on Harborview, reported that people were also illegally standing on the bridge that separated the harbor from the coastal cliff side of the town. Having decided she didn't have the manpower or jail space to arrest everyone and understanding how this could hopefully be a once-in-a-lifetime event, she made the decision to close the bridge to car traffic.

Less than two hours after Adam had told Meghann about the plan, she heard drumming and everyone turned as a group of Native Americans danced toward the harbor, clad in hawk feather headdresses and colorful ceremonial robes adorned with beads, fur, bones, and porcupine quills. Some of the men were wearing what looked like fancy feather dusters tied to their backs while women had small cone-shaped tins that jingled as they moved.

"Wow!" Emma said, starting to dance herself.

"Wow, indeed," Meghann agreed, moved by the sight. Following the dancers were men carrying three canoes. Adam had explained that given their belief that the Orca was a senior member of the tribe returned in spirit, they'd been given the honor of leading the hopefully successful procession out to sea.

There'd been a bit of argument earlier about naming the Orca, who, it turned out, hadn't yet been given an official name, just an identification number. Dee, who was wearing a hand-knitted sweater with a stylized whale design, had pushed for Captain. When Adam carefully explained that while in the old days names had been assigned by appearance or whim, they were now related to where a whale had been seen swimming, Emma loudly insisted it should be named Castaway, because it had come to her home before moving on to the harbor.

The consensus name ended up Captain Castaway, or C.C. for short, which seemed to satisfy everyone. No one thought to ask the Orca for its opinion.

The minute the first canoe hit the water, the killer whale now known as C.C. stopped wailing and swam over to it, swung his tail beneath the water and rested his chin on the side of the canoe, his big pink tongue lolling out.

One of the men in the canoe leaned down and spoke in his native language to the Orca, who seemed to be listening.

Suddenly, C.C. dove beneath the water again, a dark shadow swimming around the boat. Then he popped back up and with his blowhole closed, exhaled out a long, slow breath that sounded exactly like someone had just sat on a joke whoopie cushion.

"I told you that's the captain!" Dee called out. "That man was always giving people raspberries."

Even as everyone laughed, from the looks many exchanged, some were wondering. As impossible as it sounded, Meghann was one of them.

12

B ECAUSE ADAM HAD recruited some of his students who served as interns in his research to help out, Meghan opted to emotionally support him from back at the harbor.

Despite an Orcas' ability to swim a hundred nautical miles in a day, the procession did not move speedily. After they'd disappeared beyond the bridge and headed through the channel leading to the sea, her only contact was reports over the *Sea Wolf*'s radio that the Orca was still with them.

From time to time, as they grew closer to the ocean, the killer whale would spook and turn back, giving the impression that something must have happened to have him run away from his pod and escape to the safer environs of Shelter Bay.

Then, as everyone held a united breath, echoing the radio's silence, Adam's voice would return, announcing that they were on the move again.

As time crawled by, Meghann suspected that the towering snow-clad Mt. Hood could erupt, spewing lava and ash into the air all over Oregon and not a single person in Shelter Bay would notice.

"His mommy will find him," Emma insisted for the umpteenth time, her voice beginning to waver. As Annie lifted the girl into her arms and hugged her tightly, Meghann remembered what Adam had told her about Emma's mother having deserted her and leaving her with Mac, who'd left the military to take care of her.

She'd obviously established a strong bond with Annie, but Meghann knew, more than most, how childhood memories could unexpectedly come creeping out of dark mental closets. Fortunately, Emma Culhane had strong family support to care for her. As, she hoped, the little whale did, as well.

She tried to be patient. She really did. But after a while, waiting for radio contact wasn't enough. She loved Adam. He hadn't been her summer crush, her teenage first love. He'd been "The One."

He still was. And would always be.

She ran over to a group of teenage boys, who were wearing Shelter Bay High School Dolphins letterman jackets. "I need to borrow a bike," she said.

They exchanged looks.

Biting back her impatience, Meghann said, "I promise I'll bring it back." She dug into the pocket of her yellow rain slicker, pulling out her billfold. She'd buy the damn bike if she had to.

"You don't have to do that," one boy said. He climbed off the red Superfly racer he'd been straddling. "Would you do me one favor?"

"Of course." She'd give him anything but her first born. Because Adam may not know it, but he already had dibs.

"Would you let me take a selfie with you, me, and the bike? My girlfriend's a huge fangirl and she'll freak out when I post it on my Facebook page."

"No problem." Meghann smiled for the phone camera, thanked him, then took off peddling.

She hadn't ridden a bike in longer than she'd driven, but this one was much more lightweight than she was used to, and really, really fast.

Fortunately it also had good braking, because after racing down Harborview and around the car barricade Kara had put up onto the pedestrian-packed bridge, living up to its name, the Superfly seemed to fly back down the other side. She was afraid for a moment she'd go flying over the handlebars and break every bone in her body. And wouldn't that be a fun way to spend Christmas?

Meanwhile, she realized the one flaw in this spur-of-the-moment decision: she'd temporarily lost contact with the radio.

But she made it over the bridge, then maneuvered around the twisting, fir tree lined road to the edge of the cliff where the channel flowed into the water. In her hurry, she accidently let the bike fall, cringing as it crashed into some dead tree limbs that must have been blown down in an old storm. But paying for a new paint job was a small price for being with Adam when he hopefully reunited C.C. with his family.

The fog had lifted enough to let some sun shine through. Raising her hand above her eyes to shield the filtered glare, Meghann looked out over the sea just as a pod of pelicans flew by in formation in front of her.

The first thing she saw was the *Kelli,* Cole Douchett's fishing boat, which had gone out earlier. And there, trailing behind him, were several bullet-shaped black forms that were definitely not cormorants. He'd found them!

The Orcas were followed by the ever-present gulls, hoping for seconds if the migrating whales decided to stop to feed. Which they didn't appear to have any intention of doing.

The sound of drumming filtered through the misty fingers of fog over the screech of the gulls. Looking back down the channel, Meghann could see the canoes. And behind that, the sleek white lines of the *Sea Wolf.* And—yay!—the solitary, misplaced C.C.

She raced down the wooden steps to the beach, waving wildly as the boat passed. Her heart lifted as if attached to a bunch of helium balloons as the Orca sped past the boat and canoes, straight toward the pod just as another whale broke away and swam toward him. When they met, they both paused.

Meghann held her breath.

What if Adam's information had been mistaken? What if this wasn't the lost C.C.'s family after all? What if they couldn't communicate?

What if the pod continued south without him?

They slowly turned on their sides, C.C.'s head resting against the fluke of the larger whale.

The canoes stopped. Adam cut the *Sea Wolf's* engine.

The only sounds were the low roar of the surf rushing in to hit against the cliff, the sea breeze whistling in the trees, the screech of the gulls.

And then the click and clack coming from the two Orcas. Obviously they were having a conversation. But could they understand each other?

Apparently they could. Because slowly, amazingly, they raised their pectoral fins in unison and froze, as if posing for a photo.

Meghann didn't know how long they held that salute. It seemed like forever. Then they rolled, diving below the water as if they were performing in a water ballet. Just as she thought it couldn't get any better, they burst up, creating a towering spray of white water, breaching in that same perfect synchrony, then went racing back to the waiting pod, which began what could only be a breaching dance of pure reunion joy.

Tears were pouring down Meghann's cheeks

as Adam, who'd anchored the research boat, came wading ashore.

"You did it!" She flung herself into his arms and was lifted off the sand. "I knew you could."

He laughed at that, kissed her, and sent her heart soaring even higher.

"I'm glad one of us did."

He put her back on the ground, his hands on the waist of her yellow jacket as he looked down at her, his expression serious.

"I have something I need to say."

"Is this where you ask me to the Snow Ball?"

"What?" He shook his head. "No. I mean, damn, yes, of course I want to take you to the Snow Ball."

"Good. Because I brought a dress that's going to knock your socks off. And other pieces of clothing as well."

"I'm looking forward to it. But this is serious."

"You obviously don't know what that dress cost," she said with a toss of her fog and sea mist crazy curled head. "I spent serious money."

"I promise to appreciate it… But here's the thing. You know how I once told you that long-distance relationships were illogical?"

"Since it was the worst night of my life, even worse than my divorce, of course I do."

"I was wrong."

"I thought we'd already agreed on that."

"I understand that your work is in New York."

"Now see, that's where you're wrong." She reached up a hand to his roughened cheek. "I can write anywhere. Which is why I've already decided to stay here in Shelter Bay."

"With me?"

Meghann loved Adam. With her entire heart and soul. But she wasn't prepared to make it that easy. He had the words. She knew he did. This time she was going to make him say them.

"Are you asking?"

He took a deep breath. "Yeah. I don't know where this is going, Meggie—"

"Fortunately, for us, one of us knows how to plot a story." Okay, maybe she didn't usually plot ahead, but she'd had years to think about this one. "You're going to ask me to marry you and I'm going to say yes, and then we'll kiss, and get married on the beach with all our friends and live in..."

She paused, realizing that she didn't know

where they'd live.

"Do you have a house? Or do you live on the *Sea Wolf*?" She could manage that. Of course, those bunks in one of the cabins would have to be turned into a proper bed. But if Adam's home was on his boat, hers would be as well. At least until the children arrived.

"Remember Whaleshead?"

"That dilapidated old whaling captain's place?" She also remembered how kids would break in, especially on Halloween because the shuttered old wooden Victorian had been rumored to be haunted.

"That's it. But it's not dilapidated anymore. I had Lucas Chaffee completely renovate it." He pointed up to a blue-and-white clapboard house perched on the cliff right above them, not far from Sax and Kara's home. "I like the irony of living in the home of a guy who used to hunt whales. Although, giving him a break, times were different back then."

"You kept the widow's walk." Could it get any better? There it was, at the very top of the house, surrounded by a white iron railing.

"Lucas insisted it created character."

"It does. And it's going to allow me to watch you come back home from the sea at the end of the day."

She went up on her toes, twined her arms around his neck and kissed him.

"Which will be the best part of every day," Adam said. When he drew her closer and kissed her back, their romance spinning out on the writer's screen in her mind was better than any fiction Meghann ever could have thought up.

"And they made a home together, with their beautiful, intelligent children in their pretty blue house overlooking the sea, and all lived happily after," she said as he scooped her up and began carrying her back to the *Sea Wolf*.

Because they had a Christmas to celebrate. A Snow Ball to attend. And a life to begin.

Together.

To keep up with publication dates and other news and for a chance to win books and other cool stuff, subscribe to the JoAnn Ross newsletter. Also connect with JoAnn at her website, Facebook, Twitter, and Pinterest.

Keep reading for a sneak preview excerpt of *A Sea Change*, the next book in the Castlelough series, coming in early 2015.

A Sea Change

A Shelter Bay/Castlelough novel

JoAnn Ross

Castlelough, Ireland

ALTHOUGH THE MICROBREWERY might be a
new addition, Brennan's Microbrewery and
Pub had been serving rebels and raiders, smug-
glers and sailors, poets and patriots since 1650.

And, Sedona Sullivan considered as she
watched a young couple share a kiss inside one
of the two snugs by the front door, lovers. The
leaded glass window kept people's behavior
reasonably sedate while the stained glass door
allowed conversations to remain private.

Whiskey bottles gleamed like pirates' booty
in the glow of brass-hooded lamps, a turf fire
burned in a large open hearth at one end of the
pub, warming against the chill of rain pelting on
the slate roof, and heavy wooden tables were
crowded onto the stone floor. Booths lined walls
covered in football flags, vintage signs, old
photographs, and in the library extension, books
and magazines filled shelves and wall racks.

The man murmured something in the woman's ear, causing her to laugh and toss hair as
bright as the peat fire. As the woman lifted her
smiling lips to his for a longer, more drawn-out
kiss, Sedona felt a stir of something that felt

uncomfortably like envy.

How long had it been since a man had made her laugh with sexy abandon? How long since anyone had kissed her like the man was kissing that pretty Irish redhead?

Sedona did some quick mental math. Finding the sum impossible to believe, she recalculated. Twenty-two months, three weeks, and eight days? Seriously?

Unfortunately, given that she was, after all, a former CPA with excellent math skills and a near-photographic memory, Sedona knew her figures were right on the money. As where those additional sixteen hours she reluctantly tacked on to the initial subtotal.

How could that be possible?

Granted, she'd been busy. After leaving a high-powered accounting career in Portland, she'd opened a bakery in Shelter Bay, Cas- tlelough's sister city on the Oregon coast. But still… nearly two years?

That was just too depressing.

Unlike last evening, when Brennan's had been crowded to the ancient wooden rafters with family members and close friends enjoying Mary Joyce and J.T. Douchett's rehearsal dinner, tonight the pub was nearly deserted, save for the lovers, three men watching a replay of a rugby match on the TV bolted to the stone wall, and an ancient man somewhere between eighty and a hundred years old who was nursing a foam-topped dark ale and singing sad Irish songs to himself.

And, of course, there was Patrick Brennan, owner, bartender and cook, whose smiling Irish eyes were as darkly brown as the fudge frosting she'd made for the chocolate groom's cake.

Which was what had brought Sedona to her ancestral homeland.

She'd met international movie star and award-winning screenwriter Mary Joyce when the Castlelough-born actress had visited Shelter Bay for a film festival featuring her movies. After Mary had gotten engaged to a former Marine who'd been pressed into service as a bodyguard, Mary had asked Sedona to make both the groom's cake and the all-important wedding cake.

Happy to play a part in her friend's wedding, Sedona had jumped at the chance to revisit the land of her ancestors.

A cheer went up as a player dressed in a

green jersey from the Ireland Wolfhounds scored against the England Saxons. After delivering her order, Patrick paused on his way back to the bar long enough to glance up at the screen, and even the old man stopped singing long enough to raise his mug before switching to a ballad celebrating a victory in some ancient, but never to be forgotten war.

Sedona was thinking that watching a game when you already knew the final score must be a male thing, when the heavy oak door opened, bringing with it a wet, brisk wind that sent her paper napkin sailing off her lap and onto the floor.

Before she could reach down and pick it up, her attention was captured by the arrival of a man she had already determined to be trouble on a hot, sexy stick.

His wind-mussed hair, which gave him the look of having just gotten out of bed, fell to a few inches above his broad shoulders and was as black as the sea on a moonless night. As he took off his black leather jacket—revealing a lean hard, well-muscled body—testosterone radiated off him in bone-weakening waves that had her glad she was sitting down.

"Well, would you look at what the night gale blew in," Patrick greeted him from behind the bar. "I thought you were leaving town."

"I was. Am," Conn Brennan clarified in the roughened, gravelly rocker's voice recognizable the world over. "I'm flying out of Shannon to catch up with the lads in Frankfurt. But I had a sudden craving for fish and chips and sure, everyone knows there's no finer food than the pub grub served up by my big brother at Brennan's."

Patrick laughed at that. "Sure, with talk like that, some would think you'd be from Blarney," he shot back on an exaggerated brogue. "So how did the party go? I assume the bride and groom enjoyed themselves?"

"The party was grand, in large part due to the music," Conn Brennan said. The infamous bad boy rocker known by the single name *Conn* to his legion of fans around the world had been dubbed "Conn of the Hundred Battles" by tabloids for his habit for getting into fights with the paparazzi.

"As for the happy bride and groom, I image they're shagging their brains out about now. The way they couldn't keep their hands off each other had the local band lads making bets on whether they'd make it to bed before consummating the nuptials."

The heels of his metal-buckled black boots rang out on the stone floor as he headed toward the bar, pausing when he almost stepped on Sedona's dropped napkin. He bent to pick it up, then, when he straightened, his startlingly neon blue eyes clashed with hers.

And held for a long, humming moment.

"Well, fancy seeing you here. I would have guessed, after the busy day you've had, that you'd be all tucked away in your comfy bed at the inn, dreaming of wedding cakes, sugar plums, and all things sweet."

He placed the napkin on the table with a dangerously sexy smile he'd directed her way more than once as he'd rocked the reception from the bandstand. When an image of a bare-chested Conn, sprawled on her four-poster bed at the inn flashed wickedly through Sedona's mind, something quivered deep in her stomach.

It was only hunger, she assured herself. Between putting the last touches on the towering wedding cake and working with the serving staff during the reception, she hadn't taken time for a proper meal all day.

"I was in the mood for a glass of wine and a late bite." Her tone, cool as wintry mist over the Burren, was in direct contrast to the heat flooding her body.

He lifted an ebony brow. "Why would you be wanting to go out in this rain? The Cooper Beech Inn has excellent room service, and surely your suite came with a mini-bar well stocked with adult beverages."

"You're correct on both counts," she acknowledged as the old man segued into "The Rare Auld Mountain Dew."

She took a sip of wine, hoping it would cool the heat rising inside her.

It didn't.

"But I chose to spend my last night in Ireland here at Brennan's instead of an impersonal hotel room. Besides, you're right about your brother's food. It's excellent."

While the pub grub menu might be more casual than her chef friend Maddy Douchett's gourmet dining, Patrick Brennan had proven to be as skilled in the kitchen as he was pulling pints. "There's also the fact that the mini bar is ridiculously expensive."

"Ah." He nodded his satisfaction. "Your parents didn't merely pass down an Irish surname, Sedona Sullivan. It appears you've inherited our Irish frugality."

"And here I thought that was the Scots."

"It's true that they've been more than happy to advertise that reputation, despite having stolen the concept from us. Same as they did the pipes, which, if truth be told, were originally intended as an Irish joke on the Scots, who, being dour people without any sense of humor, failed to get it."

"And didn't I recognize your famed Irish frugality the moment you roared into town in that fire-engine red Ferrari?"

He threw back his head and laughed, a rich, deep, sound that flowed over her and reminded her yet again exactly how much time had passed since she'd been with a man.

Your choice.

"And wouldn't you be a prime example of appearances being deceiving, Sedona Sullivan?" he countered.

"Don't be disturbing my guests, Conn," Patrick called out.

"We're just having a friendly conversation."

Conn's eyes hadn't left Sedona's since he'd stopped at the table. "Am I disturbing you, *a stór*?"

Yes.

"Not at all," she lied.

The truth was that she'd been feeling wired and edgy from the moment he strode into the hall for a sound check before the reception.

"Though you do force me to point out that I'm no one's *darling*," she tacked on. He'd undoubtedly used the generic endearment the way American men used "babe" or "sweetheart."

Even without having read about all the rich and famous women the rocker was reported to have been involved with, any sensible woman would keep her distance from Conn Brennan. Despite having grown up in a commune of former hippies and flower children, Sedona had always considered herself unwaveringly sensible.

Her knowledge of the endearment failed to put a dent in his oversized male ego. Instead, amusement danced in his electric blue eyes.

"Would you have learned that bit of Irish from some local lad attracted by your charms?" he asked as he rubbed a jaw darkened with a day-old stubble that added machismo to his beautiful face. "Which, may I say, despite your short time in our fair village, would not surprise me in the least."

"My parents believe everyone should speak at least two languages," she responded mildly. "I'm fluent in Spanish, know enough just French to order a baguette and wine in Paris, and thanks to a year studying abroad at Trinity College Dublin, along with the past few days having an opportunity to practice, I can carry on a bit of a conversation in Irish."

Raindrops glistened in his black hair as he tilted his head. "Mary wasn't exaggerating when she was going on about your charms," he said finally. "And aren't brains and beauty an enticing combination? As for you not being my *darling*, Sedona Sullivan, the night's still young."

"Perhaps not for those in Dublin or Cork," she said, struggling against the seductive pull of that smile. The rugby game ended with a score by the redshirted Saxons. The men who'd been watching the TV shuffled out, muttering curses about allegedly blind referees. "But if you don't leave soon, you won't be able to drive your fancy 'frugal' import to the airport because Castlelough's cobblestone streets will have been rolled up."

He gave her a longer, considering look, his intense blue eyes narrowing as he scrutinized her in silence for what seemed like forever, even as some part of her brain still managing to function told her must have only been a few seconds.

"You're order's up," he said, without having even glanced toward the bar. "Since Patrick's occupied with my fish and chips, I'll bring your late bite back with my ale."

He smelled so amazing, like night rain darkened with the scent of leather and the tang of sweat from having played as hard for a small-town home crowd of a hundred wedding guests as he had to his recent sell-out crowd of ninety thousand in London's Wembley Stadium.

Tamping down a reckless urge to lick his dark neck, Sedona forced a slight smile.

"Thank you. We certainly wouldn't want your fish to burn while your brother's distracted delivering my meal."

Assuring herself that there wasn't a woman on the planet who'd be capable of not checking out the very fine butt in those dark jeans, she watched his long, lose-hipped outlaw's stride to the bar.

Not wanting to be caught staring as she he returned with his dark ale and her plate, she turned her gaze back to the couple in the snug. The woman was now sitting on the man's lap as they tangled tonsils.

Why didn't they just get a damn room?

"Now there's a pair who know how to make the most of a rainy night," Conn said as he sat down across from her.

There was no way she was going to respond to that.

Instead, she turned her attention to the small white plate of deep-fried cheese served on a bed of salad greens with a side of dark port and berry sauce. The triangular piece of cheese that had been fried in a light-as-a-feather beer batter nearly made her swoon.

As she'd discovered when making her cakes, Irish dairy farmers seemed to possess a magic that churned milk into pure gold. "This is amazingly delicious."

"The French claim they make the best cream and butter, but I'd put ours against theirs any day. That St. Brigid's cheese you're eating is a local Camembert from Michael Joyce's farm."

Michael was Mary Joyce's older brother. Sedona had met the former war correspondent turned farmer and his American wife at a dinner at the Joyce family home her first night in Castlelough.

"And speaking of delicious, I'm remiss in not telling you that your cake had me tempted to lick my plate."

"Thank you." When his words brought back her earlier fantasy of licking his neck, she felt color rising in her cheeks.

"Of course, I wouldn't have," he continued, thankfully seemingly unaware of her wicked, too tempting thoughts. "Because I promised Mary."

"You promised Mary you wouldn't lick your dessert plate?"

"No. Despite being an international movie star, Mary can be a bit of a stickler for propriety. So I promised to behave myself."

He waited a beat, just long enough to let her know something else was coming. "Which was the only reason I didn't leave a set to the lads and dance with you at the reception."

"Well, no one can fault you for your confidence."

"Would you be saying you wouldn't have

given me a dance? If I hadn't been performing and had asked?"

Dance with this man? From the way he'd watched her from the bandstand, his eyes like blue flames, Sedona had a feeling that dancing wasn't precisely what he'd had in mind.

"I came here to work," she said. "Not dance." Nor hook up with a hot Irish musician.

"It was a grand cake," he said. "Even better than the one I was served at the White House." Where he'd received a presidential medal for his social activism, Sedona remembered. "And one of the few that tasted as good as it looked. Most cakes these days seem to have Spackle spread over them."

She laughed at the too true description. "That's fondant, which creates a smoother surface to decorate."

"It's shite is what it is. When I was growing up, my mam's carrot cake always won first prize at the count fair. With six children in the family, we'd all have to wait our turn to lick the bowl or she'd never have ended up with enough frosting to cover it, but I always believed that the cream cheese frosting was the best part."

Sedona was relieved when Patrick arrived at

the table with his brother's fish and chips, interrupting a conversation that had returned to licking.

"Something we can agree on," she said, dipping the cheese into a sauce brightened with flavors of ginger, orange, and lemons. "Which is why I used buttercream on the cakes for the wedding."

He bit into the battered cod. Heaven help her, somehow the man managed to make chewing sexy. "So," he said, after taking a drink of the dark Brian Boru Black Ale microbrew. "Mary tells me you make cupcakes back in America."

"My bakery, *Take the Cake*, specializes in cupcakes, but I've also added pies."

"Good business move," he said with a nod. "Who wouldn't be liking a nice warm piece of pie? Cakes are well enough, but pies are sexy."

Said the man who obviously had sex on the mind. Unfortunately, he wasn't alone. As she watched him bite into a chip, she found herself wondering how that black face scruff would feel on her breasts. Her stomach. And lower still.

"Well, they're proven popular," she said as her pulse kicked up. "Which was rewarding, given that it proved the validity of months of research."

He cocked his head. "You researched whether or not people liked pie?"

"Well, of course I already knew they liked pie. I merely did a survey and cost analysis to calculate the cost and profit margins."

"Which told you lots of people like pie."

He was laughing at her. She could see it in his eyes. "Yes. Do you realize how many businesses fail on any given year? Especially these days?" They were finally in a conversational territory she knew well.

"Probably about as many people who don't succeed in the music business," he guessed. "Though I've never done a study before writing a song."

"That's different."

"Is it, now?"

"What if you wrote a song that didn't connect with your fans?"

He shrugged and took another bite of battered cod. "I'd write it off as a mistake and move on. No risk, no reward. I tend to go with my gut, then don't look back."

"My father's the same way," she murmured,

more to herself than to him.

He leaned back in the wooden chair and eyed her over the rim of his glass. "And how has that worked out for him?"

"Very well, actually."

He lifted the glass. "Point made."

"Different strokes," she argued.

"You know what they say about opposites." His gaze moved slowly over her face, his eyes darkening to a stormy, deep sea blue as they settled on her lips, which had parts of her tingling that Sedona had forgotten could tingle.

"I have a spreadsheet," she said.

"I suspect you have quite a few." When he flashed her a slow, badass grin she suspected had panties dropping across several continent, Sedona sternly reminded herself that she'd never—ever—been attracted to bad boys.

So why had she forgotten how to breathe?

As that fantasy of him sprawled in her bed next door in the Copper Beach Inn came crashing to the forefront of her mind, Sedona thought of those twenty-two months, three weeks, eight days and sixteen, no almost seventeen hours.

Even if she hadn't been coming off a very

long dry spell, every instinct she possessed told her that not only was Conn Brennan trouble, he was way out of her league.

"They're not all business related. I also have one for men."

Putting his ale down, he leaned across the small round table and tucked a strand of blonde hair, which had fallen from the tidy French twist she'd created for the reception, behind her ear. The brush of his fingertips, roughened from guitar strings, caused heat to rise beneath the erotic touch.

"You put us men in boxes." His eyes somehow managed to look both hot and amused at the same time.

It was not a question. But Sedona answered it anyway. "Not men. Attributes," she corrected. "What I'd require, and expect, in a mate."

Oh, God. Why did she have to use that word? While technically accurate, it had taken on an entirely different, impossibly sexy meaning. Desperately wanting to bury her flaming face in her palms, she remained frozen in place as his treacherous finger traced a trail of sparks around her lips, which, despite Ireland's damp weather, had gone desert dry.

"And where do I fit in your tidy little boxes, Sedona Sullivan?"

Although she was vaguely aware of the couple leaving the snug, and the pub, his steady male gaze was holding her hostage. She could not look away.

"You don't."

"I'm glad to hear that," he said on that deep, gravelly voice that set off vibrations like a tuning fork inside her.

Conn ran his hand down her throat, his thumb skimming over her pulse, which leaped beneath his touch, before cupping her jaw. "Because I've never been comfortable fenced into boundaries."

And growing up in a world of near-absolute freedom, Sedona had never been comfortable without them. "There's something you need to know."

"And that would be?"

"I'm not into casual sex."

"And isn't that good to hear." He lowered his mouth to within a whisper of hers. "Since there'd be nothing casual about how you affect me."

She drew in a sharp breath, feeling as if she

were standing on the edge of the towering cliff where J.T. and Mary's wedding had taken place in a circle of ancient stones.

"I'm taking you back to your room."

Somehow, her hand had lifted to his face. "Your flight…"

He parted her lips with the pad of his thumb. "It's my plane. It takes off when I'm ready." His other hand was on her leg, his fingers stroking the inside of her thigh through the denim of the jeans she'd put on after returning to her room after the reception. "I'll ring up the pilot and tell him I'll be leaving in the morning."

Then his mouth came down on hers and Conn was kissing her, hard and deep, setting off a blind-blinding supernova inside her.

They left the pub, running through the soft Irish rain into the inn next door. As the old fashioned gilt cage elevator cranked its way up to her floor, he continued to kiss her breathless, making Sedona forgot that she'd never, *ever*, been attracted to bad boys.

Other Books from JoAnn Ross

The Shelter Bay
(Castlelough's sister city) series:

The Homecoming

One Summer

On Lavender Lane

Moonshell Beach

Sea Glass Winter

Castaway Cove

Christmas in Shelter Bay
(Cole and Kelli's pre-novella in A
Christmas on Main Street)

You Again

Other books in the Castlelough series:

A Woman's Heart

Fair Haven

Legends Lake

Briarwood Cottage

The Shelter Bay spin-off Murphy Brothers
Trilogy:

River's Bend

About The Author

When *New York Times* bestselling contemporary romance author JoAnn Ross was seven years old, she had no doubt whatsoever that she'd grow up to play center field for the New York Yankees. Writing would be her backup occupation, something she planned to do after retiring from baseball. Those were, in her mind, her only options. While waiting for the Yankees management to call, she wrote her first novella—a tragic romance about two star-crossed Mallard ducks—for a second grade writing assignment.

The paper earned a gold star. And JoAnn kept writing.

She's now written around one hundred novels (she quit keeping track long ago) and has been published in twenty-six countries. Two of her titles have been excerpted in *Cosmopolitan* magazine and her books have also been published by the *Doubleday*, *Rhapsody*, *Literary Guild*, and *Mystery Guild* book clubs. A member of the Romance Writers of America's Honor Roll of best-selling authors, she's won several awards.

Although the Yankees have yet to call her to New York to platoon center field, JoAnn figures making one out of two life goals isn't bad.

Currently writing her Shelter Bay and River's Bend series set in Oregon, where she and her husband grew up, and her Castlelough Irish series—from where her grandparents emigrated and one of her favorite places to visit—JoAnn lives with her husband and two rescued dogs (who pretty much rule the house) in the Pacific Northwest.

Visit JoAnn's Website

http://www.joannross.com/

Like JoAnn on Facebook

https://www.facebook.com/JoAnnRossbooks

Follow JoAnn on Twitter

https://twitter.com/JoAnnRoss

Follow JoAnn on Goodreads

www.goodreads.com/author/show/31311.JoAnn_Ross

Follow JoAnn on Pinterest

http://pinterest.com/JoAnnRossBooks

Made in the USA
San Bernardino, CA
30 December 2015